Praise for *Crazy in Poughkeepsie*

"Daniel Pinkwater's new novel is a magical 'bombination,' which is to say a slow hum that starts soft and then wraps around you with snappy wit and ghostly music that makes you dance. It's a hum that gathers all together—short, tall, odd, activist, artist, teen and guru—until you realise that you're at the party of your life."
—Jewelle Gomez, author of the Gilda Stories

"The Pinkwaterverse is a place of delight and camaraderie, wordplay and weirdness, magic and epic sojourns. Each Pinkwater novel is a novelty and unmistakably part of his vast literary legacy. *Crazy in Poughkeepsie* is a trip to whale heaven, an afterlife that we can all aspire to."
—Cory Doctorow, author of *Little Brother*

"*Crazy in Poughkeepsie* is a ludicrous romp reminiscent of the Muppets! Weirdness is positive, wonderful, and everywhere in Pinkwater's writing. This is a book that will make you laugh, grin, and maybe look for more whimsy

in your own world."
—Beth Cato, author of *The Clockwork Dagger*

"Opening the pages of Crazy in Poughkeepsie was like buying a ticket back to the all the weirdness and wonder of being a kid. I'm pretty sure we passed the Phantom Tollbooth during the road trip!"
—Jacqueline Carey, author of *Starless*

Praise for *Adventures of a Dwergish Girl*

"*Adventures of a Dwergish Girl* is a book with every single thing I love about Pinkwater novels. Reading Daniel Pinkwater—as a kid and as an adult—was hugely important to my development as a writer and a human being. Meeting another Pinkwater fan is always a sign that you are among good people."
—Cory Doctorow, author of *Little Brother*

"Captivating, cool, and crazy! This story is an inspiration to us all: Be brave. Have adventures. And, most importantly, follow your dreams."
—Sam Lloyd, author of *Mr. Pusskins*

"Zany characters and a heroine with a taste for adventure fill the pages of this charming middle grade novel. Dwerg life is not for Molly O'Malley, who decides to 'skedaddle' from their quaint village hidden in the woods to find excitement in the big city. With touches of magic, conversations with ghosts, and a dash of danger in the form of gold-stealing gangsters, *Adventures of a Dwergish Girl* is sure to delight."
—Alane Adams, author of the Legends of Orkney series

"Richly drawn, quirky, and mysterious, Daniel Pinkwater's *Adventures of a Dwergish Girl* pulls readers into a dazzling adventure, complete with android Redcoats, urban magic, and, of course, the very best pizza New York City has to offer. Molly O'Malley, who might or might not be a magical Dwarf, and who might or might not be related to the folks who knocked out Rip Van Winkle for two decades, leaves behind her peaceful Catskills village and traditional expectations for females of Dwergish heritage. In true Pinkwater style, madness, mayhem, and metaphor ensue as Molly forges ahead, discovering her true strengths and pursuing her destiny.

And fleshy androids programmed to commit arson—don't forget them. After all, one should never forget to watch out for homicidal androids! Readers of all ages will enjoy this slightly twisted modern folktale as it celebrates history, strong women, and the magic of modern life."
—Susan Vaught, author of *Footer Davis Probably Is Crazy*

"*Adventures of a Dwergish Girl* by Daniel Pinkwater has that rare sense of wonder that makes you feel as if you have entered into a magical kingdom. So few writers have this knack, and it appears to come effortlessly to Mr. Pinkwater. I was delighted to jump into one of his amazing worlds."
—Joe R. Lansdale, author of *Of Mice and Minestrone*

"*Adventures of a Dwergish Girl* has a strong voice which, I admit, is Pinkwater's voice and much the same in all of his books but I never get tired of it. It's also packed full of Pinkwater's usual run of weird and quirky characters. The end teases a continuation of the story, and should that come to pass I would absolutely love

it. Highly recommended. I'm going to buy a hard copy when it's published so I can throw it at my nephew when he's old enough to appreciate it."
—*Welcome to Camp Telophase*

Other titles by Daniel Pinkwater

Young Adult

Wingman (1975)

Lizard Music (1976)

The Last Guru (1978)

Alan Mendelsohn, the Boy From Mars (1979)

Yobgorgle: Mystery Monster of Lake Ontario (1979)

The Worms of Kukumlima (1981)

The Snarkout Boys and the Avocado of Death (1982)

Young Adult Novel (1982)

The Snarkout Boys and the Baconburg Horror (1984)

Borgel (1990)

The Education of Robert Nifkin (1998)

The Neddiad: How Neddie Took the Train, Went to Hollywood, and Saved Civilization (2007)

The Yggyssey (2009)

Adventures of a Cat-Whiskered Girl (2010)

Bushman Lives! (2012)

Adventures of a Dwergish Girl (2020)

Series

The Hoboken Chicken Emergency

The Hoboken Chicken Emergency (1977)

Looking for Bobowicz: A Hobo-

ken Chicken Story (2004)

The Artsy Smartsy Club (with Jill Pinkwater, 2005)

Magic Moscow

The Magic Moscow (1980)

Attila the Pun: A Magic Moscow Story (1981)

Slaves of Spiegel: A Magic Moscow Story (1982)

Mrs. Noodlekugel

Mrs. Noodlekugel (2012)

Mrs. Noodlekugel and Four Blind Mice (2013)

Mrs. Noodlekugel and Drooly the Bear (2015)

The Werewolf Club (with Jill Pinkwater)

The Magic Pretzel (2000)

The Lunchroom of Doom (2000)

The Werewolf Club Meets Dorkula (2001)

The Werewolf Club Meets the Hound of the Basketballs (2001)

The Werewolf Club Meets Oliver Twit (2002)

Collections:

Young Adults (1991)

5 Novels (1997)

4 Fantastic Novels (2000)

Once Upon a Blue Moose (2006)

Crazy in Poughkeepsie
Daniel Pinkwater

Tachyon • San Francisco

Illustrations by Aaron Renier
Interior and cover design by Elizabeth Story

Tachyon Publications LLC
1459 18th Street #139
San Francisco, CA 94107
415.285.5615
www.tachyonpublications.com
tachyon@tachyonpublications.com

Series editor: Jacob Weisman
Project editor: Jaymee Goh

Print ISBN: 978-1-61696-374-3
Digital ISBN: 978-1-61696-375-0

Printed in the United States by Versa Press, Inc.

First Edition: 2022
9 8 7 6 5 4 3 2 1

CRAZY in Poughkeepsie

THE PLANET IS DOOMED

DANIEL PINKWATER

Illustrated by
Aaron Renier

1.

When I got home from summer camp I found a little old man stretched out on the spare bed in my room. On the other bed, my bed, fast asleep, was a skinny, shaggy dog, all angles and tufts of fur, with a long snout. The little old man was reading one of my brother's comic books, and the dog was drooling on my bedspread.

"Look, Mick! Your new roommate!" my father said.

"And his dog!" my mother said. "You've always wanted a dog."

I will explain in a little while why this statement was ironic.

I was not expecting this, neither the old man nor the dog. No one had prepared me, or told me anything. My parents obviously knew about it and had said nothing to me. They were all smirks and chuckles, as though it was an extra-nice surprise. My brother knew about it. It was clearly his doing. He was beaming with pride, as though he had brought off something wonderful.

"It's the guru!" Maurice said.

"The guru?"

"This is the guru I went to the Indo-Tibetan border to find! Guru Lumpo Smythe-Finkel, meet my little brother, Mick," my brother said.

"It's cool with you if Lhasa and I crash in your room, isn't it?" the Guru asked.

"Lhasa is the dog's name? What is it, a collie?"

"She's a Kali. It's an old Tibetan breed."

"The Guru almost didn't come with me," my brother said. "Lhasa was off somewhere, and he refused to leave his cave because he was waiting for Lhasa to come home."

"Lhasa come home?"

"That's right."

"It's fish sticks for dinner tonight," my mother said.

My brother, Maurice (pronounced, 'MAW-

2

riss,' and not 'Mo-REECE'), is an average and standard older brother. I love him, of course, he's my brother, but there's nothing particularly unusual or interesting about him, except that he took a trip to the Himalayas to find a guru. Maurice had a heavy fascination with Dr. Jiva. This was a character in a not particularly popular comic book. Maurice collected every issue, going back to number one, and had three rare and hard-to-get posters on the walls of his room. He dressed up as Dr. Jiva for Halloween. Dr. Jiva had special powers. He could read minds, cause solid objects to float up into the air, and hold his breath for fifteen minutes. He could do these things because he had been the pupil of a mystical guru who was two hundred years old and lived in a cave high up in the Himalayan Mountains.

So naturally, Maurice wanted to find a mystical guru too, so he could be more like his hero. He had dropped out of community college after one semester and was working full time as a kibbler so he could save up money for the trip. Maurice did his kibbling at Katz's Kosher Kibble Kompany, which is owned by our family and is the maker of Katz's Kosher Kitty Kibble, and Katz's Kosher Kute Puppy Kibble. Some explanation is in order here, so I will say that if you look up "kibble," the best definition you will find is, "something that has been kibbled." It is chunks or bits, usually of grain, for use as animal feed, and it comes in bags. "Kosher" refers to food that has been prepared in a manner according to Jewish law. There is no evidence that any cats or dogs belong to a specific religion, including Judaism, so it is highly unlikely that whether or not kibble is kosher would mean anything to them. Also, it is unclear whether kibble can even be kosher. To be precisely correct, the wording on the label should be in quotes, KOSHER, or better, KOSHER STYLE. Nobody seems to care.

This is why my mother mentioning that I have always wanted a dog was ironic. You would think a kid who belongs to a family that owns a dog food company would have a dog, wouldn't you? My parents explained that they liked dogs, but it's hard to keep a completely neat and clean house with pets in it. Apparently the Guru's dog, Lhasa, was all right, but she was his dog, not mine, and didn't even seem to be very interested in me.

Before his trip to Asia, Maurice was always on the lookout for a mystical guru in the neighborhood. He would ask anyone who came from the general vicinity of the Himalayas if they knew of one, and also ask anyone who looked to him as though they might have. This included people from India, Tibet, Sri Lanka, Pakistan, and also Mexico, Puerto Rico, and Hawaii. I believe most of these people were frightened by my brother.

Our father paid Maurice a miserable wage, and even though he lived at home and saved every dime, it was going to take him a very long time to get to India.

Then our great-aunt Elizabeth died. This was someone we had never met. She died and left each of us, Maurice and me, three thousand eight hundred and seventy-six dollars.

"I'm going to India," he told me. "I'm going to buy a ticket to Darjeeling, and then I'm going trekking."

"What's trekking?"

"It's walking. I'm going to trek up into the mountains."

"And look for a guru."

"That's the general idea."

6

"And you're inviting me to come with you."

"Of course, I would love that, but Mom and Dad are going to make you put your three thousand eight hundred and seventy-six dollars in an interest-bearing account, so you can apply the money to college."

"What if I don't plan to go to college?"

"Doesn't matter. You're a minor, and they can make you do whatever they want."

"What about you? You're a minor yourself."

"I finished high school, and I'm working at a job. In this family, that makes me an adult, and I can do what I like with my money. The parents and I had a big discussion about all this."

"So you get to go on a cool adventure, I get to put my inherited money in some bank."

"Ah, but I saved the good part for last. You get to go to summer camp."

"Summer camp?"

"Swimming, hiking, canoeing, crafts, archery, nature study, wood lore, and Mom and Dad are paying for it, won't cost you a cent."

"Summer camp? Have you ever been to summer camp?"

"No, but it's a great idea. I argued if I get to take a trip, you deserve something, too. Summer

camp is fun and educational."
  "Crafts? Nature study? Archery?"
  "You're going to love it, buddy."
  "Wood lore? What's wood lore?"

2.

M r. McShwartz, who teaches phys ed at my school, was friends with my father—not close friends, they had their hair cut in the same barber shop or something like that. In the summer, Mr. McShwartz and his wife ran a summer camp, Camp Hakawakaha, and he showed my father a printed brochure with color pictures. Then, one evening after supper, Mr. McShwartz came to the house. He had with him a long bulky object that turned out to be a screen, like a movie screen, that unrolled like a window shade and stood on wobbly tripod legs that folded out. He was also struggling with a thing that looked like an odd-shaped suitcase, which turned out to contain a slide projector; you put these little transparent color pictures into it, and a bright light projected them through a lens onto the screen. We turned off the living room lights, Mr. McShwartz switched on the slide projector, and he showed us scenes from Camp Hakawakaha. Slide projectors are old tech now. They used to be popular. From the clothes the kids in the pictures wore, and their haircuts, and the weird brighter-than-real color, I got the impression that the pictures had been taken a long time ago.

Listening to Mr. McShwartz talk with my father, I found out that Hakawakaha was a pretty old camp, and it had gone out of business in 1959 because of some kind of ghost scare. It was abandoned, forgotten, and falling apart. Mr. McShwartz got it cheap because it was all overgrown with weeds and poison ivy, some of the buildings were ready to collapse, and the lake was mostly dried up.

Mr. McShwartz fixed up the old camp. He hired a guy to come in with a machine called a brush hog, like a giant lawn mower, and clear out the thick undergrowth, weeds, and young trees. Then he slapped paint on the wooden buildings, got rid of most of the mouse nests from inside the cabins and most of the snakes from under them, sprayed for bugs, mopped goo on the roofs to keep them from leaking, and tacked patches on the camp canoe—not that it would ever be used. To get to what was left of the lake you'd have to drag the canoe through a quarter mile of gumbo mud and quicksand. During the cleanup, Mr. McShwartz had rummaged around in the office, found the projector and a box of color slides from the year 1957, and was ready to get people like my parents to send their kids to Hakawakaha for the summer vacation of their lives.

So while my brother Maurice was on an airplane heading for northern India, I was on a bus with a lot of other kids heading for Lake Hakawakaha.

I have to say, I loved the place. It was the first time I had ever been away from home. I loved being away from home. It's not that my parents aren't nice or that I don't get along with them. It's nothing like that. It's like this: there are clear, see-through plastic slipcovers on our living room furniture. The idea is that with the plastic covers, the furniture will stay fresh and new, never get dusty, or have anything spilled on it. The plastic covers are meant

to come off when important visitors come . . .
like maybe the Queen of England. My parents
don't know the Queen of England, or anyone
else important enough to rate removing the
covers. The plastic covers don't mean my parents are bad people, or that living at home is
unbearable torture, but staying in a place without plastic covers, or upholstered furniture, or
even glass in the windows, made me feel comfortable and also free. I hadn't ever thought
about it, but now I knew that if it were up to
me, I would never have plastic furniture covers, and one day it would be up to me. Being
away at camp let me realize that I was my own
person, different from the family I lived with,
and could have tastes and ideas that were mine
alone. That might have been enough to make
me love Camp Hakawakaha, even if there were
no other reasons . . . but there were. The food
was great! Mrs. McShwartz was famous for her
"bottomless pot" of mashed potatoes, and she
made scrumptious fried fish sticks too. I suppose this says more about the cooking at my
house than the cooking at camp, but I really
liked those fish sticks.

Mr. McShwartz was a nice guy. He took us

on hikes, and even though the lake was a half-dried-up stinking mudhole, we got to go swimming in a cattle tank on a nearby farm. Mr. McShwartz had a tractor, and he took us there on a sort of flat platform on wheels he could drag with it. We had nature study, specializing in snakes and unusual insects, and crafts, and campfires and sing-alongs. I'm not saying that Hakawakaha was a great camp, but it was everything a camp needs to be.

The other campers were all boys from my school, so I more or less knew everyone. It was a boys-only camp. Mr. McShwartz explained that he had nothing against the idea of girls, but they tended not to be as strong as boys, physically, and he wanted to avoid fatalities, or at least keep them to a minimum. There were fifteen of us. The most unusual campers were a set of triplets, the Greenwald brothers, all of whom had red hair. The brothers' favorite thing at camp was campfires. They really loved those, maybe too much. They started campfires all day long, and it was suspected they were responsible for campfiring one of the unused cabins. Two of the campers were Mr. McShwartz's sons, Nelson and Eddie. They didn't have a choice, they had to be at camp. It was hard to tell if they were really happy about it. They spent a lot of time lying around, reading. My best friend at camp was Vern Chuckoff. He had the bunk next to mine. Vern was intellectual and religious. He was also generally depressed and pessimistic. He believed the human race was doomed, a meteor was going to collide with Earth, and before that happened, a succession of corrupt government officials were going to sell the country out, and we'd all be slaves to a foreign power. Vern saw the negative side of everything, never told a joke or laughed at one, and was no good at sports. He was great, however, at telling scary ghost stories at the campfire, and he took over the job from Mr. McShwartz, who was just too pleasant and good-natured to be really frightening. Vern would dress up as a Native American, and took the name Chief Monolulu. He

made up the stories on the spot. They were about maniacs lurking in the woods, man-eating bears, and killer ghosts, and he told them in such a sad voice that we felt chills run up our spines. "And then, the ghost of the pioneer girl who died in these very woods put an end to their social security pensions, and the old people starved to death." Hakawakaha wouldn't have been Hakawakaha without Vern.

The two weeks of camp came to an end. It felt sudden. I didn't want it to be over. I wanted to stay with my friends. I wanted to lie in my bunk and hear the owl at night. I wanted to be covered in mosquito bites. Even though my mother bought the same brand of frozen fish sticks, they wouldn't taste as good at home as they did in the woods. But I had to go. My father had paid for two weeks, and two weeks were up. Mr. McShwartz put me on the bus, and I left dear old Hakawakaha behind.

3.

While I was at camp, Maurice was wandering around the border territory among the high mountains. Telling the story later, it came out that he hadn't known what country he was in. It could have been Sikkim, or Bhutan, or Nepal. Maybe he was in Tibet. Just before I left for camp, we got one postcard. It had a picture of the Happy Valley Tea Garden, and Maurice had written, "Tea! Yum!" and signed his name.

When I came home from camp, I was prepared to be bored and unhappy. I missed camp already, and the rest of the summer was going to be miserable. I felt as gloomy as Vern Chuckoff—actually gloomier, since Vern's parents had signed him up for an additional two weeks. He'd be telling ghost stories around the campfire while I was trying to choke down my mother's fish sticks at our dining table with the plastic cover on it.

There was the family car waiting for me when I got off the bus, but neither my mother nor my father were in it. Behind the wheel was my brother, Maurice!

"You're back!" I said.

"I'm back," Maurice said.

"How was camp?" Maurice asked me.

"Pretty good. How were the Himalayas?"

"Steep."

"Did you find what you were looking for?"

"Oh, I found it. Found him, I should say."

"So you must be really happy."

"I'll tell you all about it later, when we have more time."

I asked him more questions, but he refused to answer them. He didn't say anything else on the drive home. He just smiled and drove the car.

4.

After a delicious fish-stick dinner, topped off with oven-fresh frozen apple pie squirted with whipped cream substitute, the Guru went up to our room to meditate, my parents settled down in our TV-watching room to look at TV, Lhasa went with them, and Maurice asked me to come out into the backyard with him.

"So, let me tell you about my trip," Maurice said.

There was a seesaw that had been there since Maurice was a little kid, and we were sitting on it, going up and down slowly, while he told his story.

"I was just making my way with my backpack, taking local buses, hitching rides on trucks or wagons pulled by yaks. I slept in farmers' barns or local shrines, and asked everyone I met if they knew of a holy man nearby. The people in those parts are used to spiritual tourists like me, and they tolerate them as best they can. They were polite and sometimes gave me some oatmeal, or stuff that reminded me of oatmeal. Most people I met told me I should go home, but I persisted. I was going to find a guru and get mystical knowledge, and maybe powers.

"And I found one. First I only heard of him. Following directions, I got closer to the neighborhood where the holy hermit was supposed to live. Then I found out the holy man's name, Guru Lumpo Smythe-Finkel, and got a general idea of where his cave was thought to be. There was no road leading to it, and no path, no track. It was overland trekking and then climbing.

The way was difficult, and the weather was dangerous. Before I was halfway there, I was half-starved, and half out of my mind. The local food didn't agree with me, besides which I didn't have any. I had been living on scallions I picked by the roadside."

"I'm curious about how you persuaded him to come home with you."

"That part was easy. It turned out that Guru Lumpo Smythe-Finkel was behind on his rent on the cave, and about to get thrown out. I offered to pay his rent, which was only about seven bucks, and suggested he could come and live with us. When I mentioned we live in Poughkeepsie, he got all interested, said he had always wanted to see Poughkeepsie."

"I'm kind of surprised he ever heard of it."

"Seems there was some kind of mystical seer who lived here in the nineteen-hundreds, and he's a big deal in the swami community."

"Well, it looks like everything turned out better than you could have hoped," I said.

"And you don't mind sharing your room with him?"

"I just spent two weeks sharing a room with six other kids, three of whom wore possible pyromaniacs, none of whom were particularly hygienic, and some of whose behavior was relatively disgusting. I don't imagine sharing with a clean old man will be a problem."

"Oh, he's quite clean."

"Besides, I like the dog, even if she's old, has no interest in me, and belongs to someone else. At least our mother can't cover her with clear plastic. But tell me, how is the mystical wisdom thing working out for you?"

"That is what I wanted to talk with you about. But first, tell me, have I been a good older brother?"

"I have friends who have older brothers, and you are no worse than theirs."

"And you appreciate all the many things I have done for you?"

"Let me think. Things you have done for me. Help me out here, I can't remember any."

"I talked the parents into letting you go to camp."

"Yes, you did. And that worked out well. OK, let's say I appreciate that."

"So if I asked you, you'd do me a big favor, and I would remember it always, and pay you back many times?"

"Not knowing what the favor is, I can only say I'd consider it."

"Take the Guru off my hands."

5.

"You want to give me your guru?"

"I'm begging you."

"But why? Isn't he teaching you how to do mystical wisdom?"

"It isn't the way I thought it would be."

"In what way is it isn't?"

"He's nothing like Dr. Jiva. He doesn't read minds or cause solid objects to float up into the air, and he can't hold his breath for fifteen minutes."

"So what does he do?"

"He meditates. That's what he does. That's what he wants to teach me. Do you know what meditating is?"

"It's sitting and thinking, isn't it?"

"No! It's sitting and not thinking! And it's monstrous boring."

"So you want me to take your place and be monstrous bored?"

"No, you never asked him to teach you anything, so you're not on the hook. Just be his friend and hang out with him a little bit."

"Won't he wonder why you're not showing up for not-thinking class?"

"I figured a way out. I told him I'm going back to college. If I sign up for a full load of courses, I can always tell him I have homework, and that's why I can't keep up with the meditation and all that stuff."

"And in return for doing you this magnificent favor, I get what?"

"Do you have a driver's license?"

"I am too young to have one, as you know."

"I have a driver's license. Also I have practically free use, within reason, of this family's spare automobile, the magnificent 1958 Buick Limited Convertible, handed down from our grandfather to our father, and still in perfect working condition after all these years."

"Continue."

"Do this thing for me, and I will drive you

where you want to go, within reason, when I am not using the Buick to go to the community college and also fro. Also, I will charge you nothing for petrol, which is European for 'gas.'"

6.

A couple of weeks went by. I got used to having the Guru as a roommate. He was a relatively clean old man, and I liked having the dog around.

"So, are you an actual mystical guru?"

"What do you think?" the Guru asked me. "Am I the real deal or not?"

"Well, I've read a couple of Maurice's Dr. Jiva comics, and you're nothing like the guru in them. He's sort of cool and has powers, can levitate and read minds and things like that, and he goes into trances and meditates."

"How do you know I don't do all those things?"

"All I've ever seen you do is read comics from Maurice's collection, and I can hear funky old-time rock 'n' roll music leaking from your headphones."

"I'll let you in on a little secret about meditation and the mystic arts," the Guru said. "You don't really use your mind for much of it, and just counting your breaths in and out gets boring. When I am in a state of deep meditation, I can enjoy reading a comic, or listening to Tuba Skinny, Leon Redbone, and the great Louis Armstrong, no problem. And I can read minds just fine. In fact, I knew you were going to ask me about this."

"How about levitating?"

"That sort of thing is for show-offs and beginners. And, for your information, I wouldn't classify the music I listen to as rock 'n' roll. Better to call it traditional jazz. Not many people know that Leon Redbone was a disciple of mine, and a good one."

"Speaking of that, wasn't Maurice supposed to be your disciple? Now he's hardly ever around. You sit around the house, reading his comics, and take walks with the dog. Weren't you supposed to be guiding and advising him?"

"I advised him to enroll in the current semester at the community college. So, between kibbling and studying he'll be pretty busy, and you may not see so much of him. When he has completed two years, he will transfer to the state university. He is going to study to become an accountant."

"That's what you advised him? That's what he learned? Any responsible adult could have suggested that."

"I'm a responsible adult."

"What about showing Maurice how to meditate, and develop mystical powers, and learn the secrets of the lamas of Tibet? Wasn't that part of the deal?"

"Your brother hasn't got the chops for it. Takes talent to be a master of the mystic arts.

Crazy in Poughkeepsie

You, on the other hand, show a lot of potential
for being a student of the ancient wisdom."
  "Thanks, not interested."
  "Just the same, you'd be good at it."

7.

In case anyone was wondering, my parents simply loved Guru Lumpo Smythe-Finkel.

"He's such a gentleman," my mother said. "And he speaks English beautifully, with hardly a trace of an accent."

"He told me he grew up in New Jersey."

"That's what I mean. He calls a fork a fork, doesn't say, "fawk," and he never says, "yo," and he's a sagacious person. It's an honor to have him stay with us."

"You didn't remove the plastic furniture covers."

"Well, it's an honor, but not a big, big honor."

"Also, how come it's OK for Lhasa to live here? You never would let me have a dog."

Crazy in Poughkeepsie

"Lhasa is special. She understands every word I say."

My father liked the Guru because he watched golf on TV with him. My father spends his Sundays watching golf—not that he plays the game, just likes to watch it. Neither my mother nor my brother nor I can bear watching golf. My father likes it, and the Guru likes it, therefore my father likes the Guru.

Just to have something to do, I started going along on walks with the Guru and Lhasa the Tibetan Kali. The Guru walks at a brisk pace. I had no problem keeping up with him, but it wasn't easy to keep up a conversation. The dog trots alongside, looking like she could do this in her sleep. Walking with Guru Lumpo Smythe-Finkel and Lhasa is good exercise. It would be fairly boring, except for little details I began to notice. These were things I never noticed walking by myself, and it almost seemed that there were things that only happened when the Guru was present. For example, I have lived in Poughkeepsie my whole life, and have practically never seen a snake. When walking with the Guru, I saw them all the time, and instead of gliding along on the ground, like snakes do,

when they'd see him coming, they'd sort of raise up their heads as high as they could, and watch him as he went past. Birds did something similar, hopping onto branches near him. Also, chipmunks and squirrels tended to stay close instead of getting out of his way. It wasn't just animals that reacted to the Guru in unusual ways—people were always greeting him and nodding to him. We saw types and varieties of people you don't necessarily see all the time, like extremely small people, and immensely fat or weirdly tall people, people wearing odd outfits, possibly the national costumes of some foreign countries . . . or planets.

The Guru never took the same route twice. We'd walk along some of the streets in the neighborhood around my family's house, but every day we'd get into some other part of town, and cover every street, even little, short, dead-end ones. It got so we'd walk a long distance to get to some area we hadn't covered before. I thought the Guru had mentally placed a grid over a mental map of the City of Poughkeepsie, and the greater Town of Poughkeepsie which surrounds it, and was planning to walk every walkable inch of the place. "Are we looking for something?" I asked the Guru. "Is this a search?"

"Sort of," he said.

"What are we looking for?"

"It's hard to explain. I'll know it when I find it."

"Can you give me a general idea?"

"I suppose you've heard of the Lost Dutch-man's Cave."

"Sure. It's a local legend. There's supposed to be a hidden river under the city. It's a myth."

"Is it?"

"Isn't it?"

"We'll know when we find it."

"So that's what we're looking for?"

"No, that's just an example. Unless it happens to turn out to be the thing we're looking for."

"And you'll know that when you find it."

"That's right."

8.

If he was feeling hungry, the Guru would pull his bowl out of the sort-of shoulder bag he carried, and say, "Take this bowl, ring the bell, and say, 'There is a holy man with me, and he is old and weak. Please give him something to eat.' Try to look cute, or cute as you can. Lhasa will go with you." I'd ring the bell, someone would come out and say, "Oh, what a nice doggie!", and sure enough, they would come up with bananas or muffins or something.

"This is begging, isn't it?" I asked the Guru. "Are we beggars? Isn't begging against the law?"

"It would be begging if we asked for stuff and didn't offer anything in return," the Guru said. "People want to give us something to repay us for what we're giving them, and we don't want to insult them by rejecting their gifts."

"Run that by me again. What is it we are giving them?"

"Happiness."

"Happiness?"

"Sure. It makes them happy to have us around."

"Let me get this straight: there's a kid, a scruffy old man, and a scruffy old dog, just kicking down the street, and this makes people happy, and they run inside their houses and make grilled cheese sandwiches for us?"

"Sure. Why not?"

"By the way, why don't you just send the dog? She's the one who closes the deal."

"Well, she knows how it's done, but then she'd bring the food to me in her mouth and get spit all over everything. She can't help drooling, she's a dog."

"So my role in this swindle is to carry stuff. It would be the same if you had a monkey."

"Some gurus have them, but they're not very sanitary either, and don't forget you're learning things all the time."

"There's something I've been meaning to ask you."

"Ask away. I am here to enlighten you."

"You were living in a cave high in the Himalayan Mountains."

"Right."

"And you came to Poughkeepsie of your own free will."

"Your brother paid for my airplane ticket, so naturally."

"Why would you want to be in Poughkeepsie? Why would anybody?"

"Oh, that was because it was my destiny. I was destined to come."

"To Poughkeepsie."

"Yes. I have known for years that I had to be in Poughkeepsie."

"Why? Why could that possibly be? I mean, I live in Poughkeepsie. It's OK. I like it well enough, but why would you, a guru from more exciting places like the Himalayas or New Jersey, have to come here? Why is it your destiny, as you put it?"

"Before I answer that, let me say that I am pleased with your progress."

"My progress?"

"As my pupil. Now to answer your question, there is something I have to do or find, here in Poughkeepsie."

"And that something is?" I asked, almost sure I knew the answer."

"I'll know it when I find it."

"Right. You'll know it when you find it."

9.

"Earlier today you said I was your pupil. How do you figure I'm your pupil?"

"You're learning things."

"I'm learning how to promote free lunches."

"And you're learning every street in greater Poughkeepsie. You'll be a cinch to get a job driving a cab, or working in the postal service, or something for the city, and at the very least you'll always know where you are."

"Do you consider this to be a mystical-guru-wisdom-of-the-East kind of thing?"

"Knowledge is knowledge. Now put out the light and let's get some sleep. We have a lot of territory to cover tomorrow."

There were a couple of old-fashioned pressed-steel chairs on our porch. These were the kind of chairs that come in different colors, have a metal seat and back, steel pipe arms, and a slightly springy base so the chairs seem to rock a little. You can't sit on them wearing shorts in hot weather because the sun will have heated the chairs to a burning temperature; likewise when it's cold, they will freeze your tuchas. They belonged to my grandparents, who bought them at Sears and Roebuck for five dollars apiece. I knew this because the price tags were still glued on the backs. You wouldn't think anyone would bother to steal one of these chairs, but someone did, or anyway tried to. Lhasa woke up barking like a maniac, shot down the stairs, and pounded on the front door with her paws. I stumbled after her, not sure what was happening, but sure it was something. When I opened the door, Lhasa shot through with a growl that turned into some serious barking. She never left the porch, just kept up an ear-piercing racket, and I could see the thief abandon the chair he had carried down to the street and run off into the night. He was laughing! He was waving his arms as he ran away!

So it was some kind of prank or goof. That made more sense than anyone wanting one of

those chairs enough to break the law to get it. It was a drunk, or a crazy person, just having some obnoxious fun. I stood there on the porch, in my pajamas, with Lhasa, who was wearing a satisfied expression. She had protected her territory, which apparently our house had become. If I had an expression, it would have been a puzzled expression. I didn't get a good look at the chair thief, but from what I could see, he appeared to be someone I knew.

But it couldn't have been. The laughing, arm-waving, crazy porch-furniture-stealing, antisocial idiot could not have been who I thought I'd seen. It could not have been the intellectual and quiet, pessimistic and polite Vern Chuckoff from camp.

My parents and brother, Maurice, were

awakened by the attempted robbery and demonstration of dog vocal power, but they arrived after the show was over. I explained it to them, and their comment was what you'd expect. They wondered why anybody would want to steal one of those chairs, which they only kept out of affection for my mother's parents, whose chairs they had been. My father's parents had left us a hideous birdbath, which went nicely with the chairs.

The Guru slept through the whole business. When I asked him how he had been able to do that, he said, "The dog handled it, didn't she? There was no reason for me to wake up."

Not only did Lhasa handle it—if handling was the same as making an incredible amount of noise—but a couple of times it almost sounded as though she had said the word "woof," instead of barking. Dogs can make a sort of "woo" sound, but their lips are such that they can't do an "f."

The very next night, there was another unusual event. A disturbance, only not noisy enough to wake the whole house, and apparently Lhasa didn't consider it a threat, so I was the only one who heard it.

"*Haha*

Crazy in Poughkeepsie

Waka
Ha
Ha
Ha
Hakawakaha, Hakawakaha
Camp camp camp camp
Svaha!"

It was the Hakawakaha camp cheer. There were a couple of voices out in the street, not loud enough to wake people up, except me. Maybe that was because I knew the cheer, and it resonated with the memory in my head. I got out of bed, went downstairs, switched on the porch light, and stepped outside. Sitting in one of the pressed-steel porch chairs was none other than Vern Chuckoff, and in the other was a girl, sort of small, with biggish hands and feet.

"Hey, Mick! This is my girlfriend, Molly."

"I'm not his girlfriend."

"Well, she's a girl and she's my friend."

"I wouldn't say I'm his friend either."

"Molly comes from the Catskill Mountains, across the river. Her family are some of those old-fashioned people who don't use electricity, and wear beards and straw hats and all that."

"That's so," Molly said. "Only it's the men who have beards. The women are cute, like me."

"By the way, I didn't know this was your house, or I would never have tried to steal the chair," Vern Chuckoff said.

"Why did you want to steal it at all?" I asked.

"I'm a juvenile delinquent is why. Molly is one, too."

"Well, the part about me is true," Molly said. "Vern is a pretty poor excuse for a delinquent."

"Molly lives in the park. She sleeps in a tree."

"It's not because I have to. I can afford to rent the fanciest apartment in Poughkeepsie, or buy a mansion if I feel like it."

"And as you can see, she's crazy. Don't you think I'm cool to have a girlfriend like this?"

"Not your girlfriend."

"OK, I'm cool that she hangs out with me."

"I hang out with a sagacious guru," I said.

At this point the Guru appeared in the doorway with Lhasa. "The dog wants scrambled eggs," he said. "Why don't you invite your friends to join us in the kitchen, and not too much noise, please."

10.

"Lest anyone think I'm taking advantage of Mick's parents' hospitality, this dozen eggs was given to us by some kind householders," the Guru said.

"We go around begging for food," I said.

"Accepting sincere tributes is not begging. I am going to prepare scrambled eggs in the traditional Tibetan style."

Traditional Tibetan style turned out to be with buttered whole wheat toast and coffee.

"It's how they made them at the monastery where I used to stay," the Guru said. "Now what is it with you kids ranging around at night, chanting and trying to make off with other people's property?"

"Yes, what is it with you, Vern? Just a few

weeks ago you were a quiet and serious kid, if a little depressing to be around."

"I met Molly," Vern Chuckoff said. "She showed me a whole new way to be. We make noise at night in residential neighborhoods, we drink wine, and as you saw, we're getting into stealing porch furniture."

"And I am crazy," Molly said. "A friend of mine told me I'd go crazy if I crossed the Hudson River and came to live in Poughkeepsie, and turns out she was right."

"Poughkeepsie is all right if you're used to it," I said. "But what prompted you to leave the majestic Catskill Mountains and come here in the first place?"

"A witch told me I had to," Molly said.

"Oh, a witch. That's right up my street," the Guru said. "I understand something about

your situation and condition. But why do you say you're crazy? What makes you think so?"

"I'm not myself," Molly said. "I say and think things I don't recognize, and I do things I never did before."

"Like sleeping in a tree?"

"No, I've always done that, off and on. I mean, being obnoxious and antisocial, waking people up, knocking over garbage cans—that was never me before."

"And this all happened when you moved to Poughkeepsie from across the river?"

"Right. When my friend suggested it would happen, but I thought she just meant I would go out of my mind with boredom living in this town."

"As many do," the Guru said. "I have a few thoughts about you kids. If you have no objection, I could share some observations with you."

"Share away," Molly said.

"I'll start with Vern," the Guru said. "He is a nice boy, but he was obviously so boring that he bored himself, and could barely stand it. He runs into Molly, who is embarking on a career as a small-time criminal nuisance, and it's a wonderful improvement, so he joins her. If

she were bungee jumping off the Mid-Hudson
Bridge, or trying to get skunks to spray her, it
would have been just as attractive."

"Can we do those things?" Vern asked. "I'm
not scared of skunks."

"Now, Molly's case is more complicated. Molly,
do you know you have a special destiny? I have
one myself, so I know what I'm talking."

"The witch may have mentioned something
about it. By the way, this was not some local
neighborhood witch. It's the Catskill Witch, the
gold standard of witchery, a well-known witch,
who's very much respected."

"Who has not heard of the Catskill Witch?"
Guru Lumpo Smythe-Finkel said. "I wouldn't
presume to add anything to her instruction, but
I might mention one thing, if you will permit."

"It would be wrong to accept a man's scrambled eggs and then refuse to listen to his advice."

"I won't say much, except that going through
a crisis is part of a certain kind of destiny; it's
normal, and you're stuck with it, for the present, anyway."

"By 'crisis,' you mean being crazy?"

"Call it that. Just don't get depressed over it.

Crazy in Poughkeepsie

It's not likely to be permanent, or if it is, you'll get used to it."

"How would you know that?"

"I'm a sagacious guru."

"Fair enough."

"How about me?" Vern Chuckoff asked. "Do you have any advice for me?"

"I do, as a matter of fact. You should find a hobby, something involving skill, something artistic, maybe."

"I was thinking of taking up graffiti."

"That would be perfect."

11.

"So can I come with you some time when you go out begging?" Molly asked.

"We don't go around specifically to beg," the Guru said. "We just beg—that is to say, allow people to contribute some food—when it's time to eat."

"I'm not sure I see the difference," Molly said.

"It's like this," the Guru said. "In this culture, the guy who owns a factory or a big company is at the top of the heap, socially and economically. But in some cultures, the guy who begs for his bread, namely the wandering monk, or lama, or as in my case, a sagacious guru, is considered the best kind of person you can be, and people like to participate and maybe pick up some good luck by making with the donations."

Crazy in Poughkeepsie

"What would you say if I were to offer you a big fat gold coin worth thousands of dollars?" Molly asked the Guru.

"I would say, 'no thanks,' but if I hadn't just enjoyed scrambled eggs, I would be very happy to accept a cheese sandwich or a slice of pie."

"Interesting."

"And now, I must call an end to this scrambled egg party," the Guru said. "Mick and I have places to go in the morning."

12.

At 8:45 every morning, the Dunk'n'Dunk on Lord Cornbury Boulevard throws out the stale and broken doughnuts from the night before, and if you go around the back and slip a buck to the employee, or if you're us, let Lhasa give out with her special irresistible look, you can go away with a bag containing a dozen assorted, in various conditions. On this particular morning, who should we meet, sitting on a garbage can behind the shop and nibbling on a cruller, but Molly?

"They have pumpkin ones," she said.

"So, you know about the best doughnut deal in Poughkeepsie," Guru Lumpo Smythe-Finkel said.

"Of course, I could buy the whole store if I

wanted," Molly said. "But I prefer doughnuts when they're just going stale."

"Crazy as a loon," I whispered to the Guru, and to Molly I said, "Is Vern Chuckoff with you this morning?"

"Vern is spray-painting slogans on an abandoned factory building," Molly said. "I'm going to bring him these doughnuts."

"Give Mick a minute to negotiate for a sack of lemon creme-filled and we'll come along with you, if we may."

"It will be an honor," Molly said.

Molly was an excellent walker. She had no problem keeping up with the Guru, and I even had the feeling she was holding back a little. Without showing off, or being obnoxious about it, she took the lead, and we went where she wanted to go.

One of the things Poughkeepsie could be famous for, if Poughkeepsie were famous, is abandoned factory buildings. Over the years, even over the centuries, there have been all kinds of manufacturing and industry, going all the way back to when dead whales were dragged up the Hudson River and cut up, processed, had their oil extracted, and maybe kibbled, for all I know. The whale-processing business was carried out seventy-five miles up the river from New York Harbor, because that way it was considered less likely that pirates would show up . . . and . . . steal the whales? It doesn't make sense to me, but they teach this in school. Various other products came from Poughkeepsie, such as decks of cards, underwear, and beer, and when any of the companies that made them moved or shut down, they'd just leave the factory to fall apart.

The most famous Poughkeepsie product was cough drops. The Smith Brothers cough drop factory opened in 1847, and the little white boxes with the pictures of the two bearded Smith Brothers were known all over the world. Not generally known is that Poughkeepsie was a center of cough-drop making before the Smith Brothers came to town. Algonquin Slippery Elm Lozenges went back to 1712, for example, and in the 19th century, any number of cough-drop factories opened in Poughkeepsie in an effort to trade on Smith Brothers's fame. There was Smooth Brothers, Beard Brothers, and Schmidt Brothers, each of which had a factory, and each of which went broke or moved away, and each factory was left abandoned.

Sometimes the abandoned factory didn't disintegrate all at once. For example, a handsome brick structure where sidesaddles for lady equestrians were made closed down when ladies stopped using those, but was taken over by another concern that made horsehair-stuffed seat cushions for wagons, and later for automobiles. Next, the building housed a firm that made wooden water buckets, and then one that specialized in umbrella handles. Each time another manufacturing business took over, the place got crummier, broken windows weren't repaired, roof leaks weren't patched, and bricks fell out of walls.

The reason I know all this is because of Mr. Hatch, my fourth-grade teacher, who was a local history enthusiast. He took our class on field trips. We'd stand among the weeds and broken pavement in what had been a parking lot and look at some pathetic former factory while he told us all about it. So I knew exactly where I was when Molly led us to what had once been Rosenblatt Brothers Churnworks, which made wooden objects like a barrel with a straight handle sticking out the top. People used to pump the handle up and down to make butter from milk or cream. Vern Chuckoff was busily decorating the brick walls of the old factory with slogans: 320,000 VIRUSES AFFECT MAMMALS; IF YOU ARE UNDER 30 THE WORLD WILL RUN OUT OF DRINKING WATER IN YOUR LIFETIME; 10 COMPANIES CONTROL ALL THE FOOD IN THE WORLD; THE EARTH IS HIT BY 6,100 METEORS EVERY YEAR; 60% OF WORLD POPULATION LIVES WITHIN 60 MILES OF THE SEA.

I was impressed by Vern's very neat printing, and how straight and parallel the lines were. He had chosen pink and pastel blue and green for his colors.

"This is just for practice," Vern Chuckoff said. "Not very many people come here, but when I get better at it, I am planning to show my work downtown, the railroad station, and a couple of water tanks."

"I had no idea you were so talented," Molly said. "Have a doughnut."

"Where did you get all the facts?" I asked Vern.

"Who did you have for fourth grade?"

"Mr. Hatch."

"I had Mr. Finnegan."

"Ah."

"What's inside this building?" Guru Lumpo Smythe-Finkel asked.

"You might not want go in there," Molly said.

"I mightn't?"

"No, and this is not because I am crazy."

"And for why might I not?"

"There are entities."

"What sort of entities?"

"Ghosts. The joint is jumping with ghosts. People are often scared of ghosts, not you of course, but I am just mentioning."

"This is interesting," the Guru said. "Do you have a lot of experience with ghosts?"

"I have tons of experience with ghosts."

"And how do you know this old and abandoned factory building has them?"

"I can hear them plain as day. They're talking and singing and carrying on. It's like Mardi Gras in there."

"Mick, do you hear anything going on inside the old churnworks?"

"I hear some pigeons, I think, but nothing more."

"Vern, how about you? Do you hear ghosts making a ruckus inside this building?"

"I hear nothing, but if there are ghosts in

there, I'm for going in and seeing them. I am not scared of ghosts of any kind."

"Also, the dog is quietly napping, and showing no particular interest one way or the other. So you, Molly, would appear to be the only one who's thinking along the lines of haunted."

"Unless you think so, too," Molly said. "I imagine a wise old guru knows when there are ghosts around."

"Since I am a wise old guru, I will defer to your tons of experience. What do you believe will happen if we enter the old building?"

"Nothing."

"Nothing?"

"We'll spook the spooks. They'll vanish in the blink of an eye. It's broad daylight. They don't want alive people catching them in the act of rocking out and singing and such. Goes against their image. Much better to come back at night, which is the more traditional time, and I suggest you let me visit first and find out if these ghosts are receptive. They may not want to meet anyone, depends on a lot of things."

"Then we'll do it your way."

"As you should."

13.

"So, what's the deal with this Molly character?" I asked Guru Lumpo Smythe-Finkel when we were alone.

"What do you mean, what's the deal?"

"I mean she gets to handle the ghosts and everything."

"Well, she's experienced."

"She's also a nutcase, by her own admission. Did you take that into account?"

"I did indeed. Sometimes, people who are cut out to become special go batty for a while—or permanently. That witch who sent her here is good. Possibly she knew Molly was supposed to meet up with some wise person in Poughkeepsie of all places, who would become her teacher. For a second I thought it might be me, and that was what my being here was all about, but the vibration wasn't there. Just as well. I have my hands full with you."

"You still think I'm your pupil."

"I'm a guru. You hang out with me every day. There's no other way to figure it."

"Apropos nothing, what's with the dog?"

"Ah, you're starting to notice stuff. Yes, she's a guru too. Knows a lot more than I do. When you develop some more, you may start to understand her. Meanwhile, make with the treats, give her ear massages and rump rubs. You want her to like you."

The next morning, behind the Dunk'n'Dunk, there was Molly, sitting on a garbage can, digging into a bag of last night's cinnamon crullers.

"I've been to see the ghosts," she said.

"And how was that?" the Guru asked.

"Hoo boy! You won't believe what goes on in that old churn factory. They've got a whale in there!"

"An actual whale?"

"It's the ghost of a whale, and may I say, it's a whale of a ghost."

"Can animals be ghosts?" I asked the Guru.

"Of course they can. I'll never understand why

people insist on thinking we have less in common with the other creatures than we do."

"They also have some hot music going on," Molly said. "Pixieland, mostly."

"Is that like Dixieland?"

"Similar, but Pixieland is more authentic. Some of the original musicians are still playing in the afterlife, you know. Anyway, the ghostly types were perfectly nice to me, but I am not invited back at this time, and neither are you, Mick. However, they would like the Guru to call at his convenience."

"I can drop up there after I knock off a couple of these Bavarian cremes," the Guru said. "Perhaps you children can wait for me in the old parking lot, and then we'll be on our way.

Molly, did you get any idea for how long the ghosts will be wanting me?"

"They said they want to tell you something, I don't have the impression it will be a long meeting. Ghosts aren't usually wordy. Above the parking lot is the water tank. Vern Chuckoff is up there painting THE PLANET IS DOOMED, and we can watch."

14.

The Guru was back with us in fifteen minutes. Vern Chuckoff was painting the second 'o' in "Doomed." He had chosen sky blue for the whole phrase.

"Those are some lively ghosts," the Guru said. "Probably more correct to say 'deadly ghosts,' but it gives a wrong impression."

"Are they still dancing and playing jazz music?" Molly asked.

"The party has been going on for months, they tell me. Maybe years. Here, Mick, I brought you this."

The Guru handed me a length of some kind of wood with holes in it. "What is it?"

"It's a flute. I need you to learn to play it, preferably in under a week."

"I'm not very musical."

"You don't know until you try. Besides it may be a magic flute. Just fool with it, you may surprise yourself, and flute-playing may be a feature when we go on our adventure."

"We're going on an adventure?"

"Don't you think it's about time we did?"

"I admit, I was wondering when we'd get started on something."

"You can't rush this stuff. Now, the ghosts who hang out in this old abandoned churn factory certainly love their pet."

"Their pet being?"

"The whale. Her name is Luna, she's a peach. I've never met a more lovable whale."

"I thought she was lovable, too," Molly said. "I take it, in life she was a victim of the whale-processing industry here in Pough-keepsie."

"Not at all," the Guru said. "Those whale-works only lasted about ten years, and went bust when petroleum was discovered in Penn-sylvania and knocked out the whale-oil busi-ness. Whales have been coming up the Hudson probably from the dawn of time. You see, the Hudson River is something called a riverine estuary, meaning it has a current that goes in two directions. Salt water pushes up from New York Harbor, and fresh water comes down from Albany and points north. The river has tides, the water is brackish in some places, fresh in others, and saltwater creatures like sharks and whales come all the way up this far."

"So, Luna, the lovable whale, who is presently dead and a ghost, was one of those whales who came up to Poughkeepsie?"

"And died," the Guru said.

"Very interesting," I said. "But didn't you say we were going on an adventure?"

"We are. Anyway, I am. I have to be away for a while, probably just a few days, and when I come back, it's adventure time for us all! I'll be in touch with Vern Chuckoff. He'll tell you what to do."

"Vern will? How come Vern? What about me, your pupil?"

"Oh, now you admit you're my pupil. Well, you have to learn to play that flute thing. It will be fine. Vern is a good boy and wants to help. Take care of Lhasa. Make sure she gets her kibble."

And then, Guru Lumpo Smythe-Finkel was gone. It was as though he had vanished into thin air. What really happened, I was pretty sure, was he just hurried out of the old and broken parking lot with weeds growing between the cracks, but he moved so fast that none of us saw him leave.

15.

Vern Chuckoff climbed down from the water tank. He had a jar of turpentine, and he was cleaning his brushes. "Where's the Guru? I thought I saw him from up there."

"He sort of vanished into thin air, sort of. He said he'd be in touch with us, through you."

"That makes sense," Vern said.

"Why does it make sense?"

"I'm the most serious one."

"Speaking of that, let me ask you a question," I said.

"Sure. Go ahead."

"When we were at Camp Hakawakaha, you were pessimistic and depressed. Then you turned up back in town, and you were getting started uu a juvenile delinquent along with Molly here."

Crazy in Poughkeepsie

"He had no talent for it," Molly put in.

"And now, you're back to being pessimistic and depressed. So what is with you?"

"I'm not pessimistic and depressed. I am the opposite of pessimistic and depressed."

"Not pessimistic and depressed? You just got finished painting 'The Planet is Doomed,' on the water tank."

"I did."

"And it's a depressing message."

"No, it's not."

"Wait, do you believe, or do you not believe that the planet is doomed?"

"As of this moment, I'd have to say yes, I believe it is doomed."

"But it's not a depressing message?"

"Not from where I'm looking at it."

"Explain."

"I'm doing something about it."

"By painting those words on a water tank."

"Correct."

"Explain some more."

"I paint the words, 'The Planet is Doomed' on the water tank. Someone comes along and sees it. You see it. 'What does that mean?' the someone asks. 'Is the planet actually doomed?'

See, now they're thinking about it. Maybe they mention it to someone else, and then there are two people thinking about it, actually three, because I was thinking about it, which is why I painted it. Next those two people bring it up in discussion with two other people, and then there are four people."

"I get it," I said. "It's that story about putting a grain of rice on the first square of a chessboard, and two grains on the next, four grains on the one after that, then eight grains, and by the time you get to square sixty-four the number of grains of rice on the board is eighteen quintillion, four hundred forty-six quadrillion, seven hundred forty-four trillion, seventy-three billion, seven hundred nine million, five hundred fifty-one thousand, six hundred and fifteen, isn't it?"

"Right, so it's pretty un-depressing that I'm getting everybody on earth to think about the problem."

"Except that the planet is still doomed."

"That can be turned around."

"How?"

"That's other people's job. I'm just pointing something out."

Crazy in Poughkeepsie

"So you're an activist."

"I'm an artist. My job was pretty much done when I picked sky blue for the lettering on the old water tank. Looks pretty good, doesn't it?"

I had to admit, it did.

16.

The Guru not being around meant I could skip the daily hike, but I didn't. When Lhasa poked her cold wet nose in my ear, and I woke up the next morning, it was as though my legs wanted to do some walking. I had gotten used to it, and now I was stuck with it. Besides, the dog was insisting. I dumped some Katz's Kosher Kute Kollie Kibble into Lhasa's bowl, and while she nibbled, I brushed my teeth and tied my sneakers. Then we hit the street.

I took along the weird wooden flute the Guru had given me. I thought I might take a break in some quiet place and practice with it. Practice would have been too strong a term—I could barely get the thing to make a noise. The Guru didn't have it with him when he went into the ghost-infested old factory, and he gave it to me when he came out. That suggested it was a ghostly flute in some way or other, and should have supernatural or sort-of magical properties, but if it had any, they did not include making it easy to get a sound out of it.

We walked along Andrew Jackson Davis Road, which took us to Lord Cornbury Boulevard about a block from Dunk'n'Dunk. That had been my plan. I went around back to negotiate for a bag of stalenuts. Vern Chuckoff was there. "I got toasted coconut crullers," he said. "And a couple plain ones for the dog. Also, I brought a thermos of hot chocolate. Let's sit on the curb and have a picnic. Then you can help me distribute these works of art."

Vern had probably two hundred sheets of paper on which he had stenciled in various colors. They all had the same thing stenciled on them: "CLIMATE CHANGE IS A REAL THING, YOU ADULT NITWIT. HELP SAVE THE PLANET."

"We'll put them under the windshield wipers on parked cars," Vern said.

There were plenty of cars parked at the railroad station, waiting for their owners to get off the train from New York City when they

came back from working there. We put a stenciled notice under the windshield wipers of
every other car. "That's all the odd-numbered
ones," Vern Chuckoff said. "We'll come back
tomorrow and do the evens."

"And Molly is the crazy one," I said.

"She is. She's crazy, I'm eccentric. Artistic
people can be eccentric. Last time I saw Molly,
she was yelling about orangutans having their
artwork stolen in the Yankee Doodle Cafeteria
on Main Street. Now that's crazy."

17.

"That's right. Those orangs are being exploited," Molly said when I asked her about it later. "Unscrupulous art dealers from New York City come up here and buy the paintings done by orangutans for cheap. Then they put bogus signatures on them, as though artists in New York had done them, and sell them in art galleries for a lot of money. The orangs don't see a dime. It's a scandal. All the zoo gives the orangs is Purina Chimp Chow, and they're allowed to watch television one hour a week."

"What zoo?" I asked. "There's no zoo in Poughkeepsie, or anywhere around here."

"Not that anybody knows about," Molly said.

"That Purina Chimp Chow is good kibble," I said. "And maybe the orangs enjoy painting.

What would they do with money?"

"It's the principle of the thing," Molly said.

We were having this conversation in Vern Chuckoff's basement. We were cutting out thin strips of paper from sheets Vern had printed with tiny slogans:

RISING TEMPERATURE KILLS FISH

POLAR ICE IS MELTING

SEA LEVELS ARE RISING STEADILY

WILDLIFE POPULATION DOWN 68% SINCE 1970

THIS IS THE ONLY PLANET YOU'VE GOT, DUMMY

"What are we doing this for?" I asked Vern.

"Fortune cookies," Vern said. He produced a huge plastic bag full of fortune cookies.

"Where'd you get those?"

"They belong to the Sha Dan Duang Palace Chinese takeout," Vern said.

"You stole them?"

"I borrowed them. They'll get them back, after we change the fortunes."

"Change the fortunes? They're baked in. How are we going to change them?"

"We remove the fortunes with the weak jokes or meaningless predictions, like 'Today is your lucky day,' and insert these important messages."

"I figured out that's what you want to do, but the question is how?"

"I happened to see a movie about how they make fortune cookies," Molly said. We both looked at her. "It was a feature film. It was a romantic comedy, and it was set in a fortune cookie factory, so it shows a lot about how they make them. The cookie is like a disc, and while it's still warm and flexible, they drop in the slip of paper with the fortune, and fold the cookie. It cools and gets hard and brittle."

"So there's no way to get the fortune out without breaking the cookie," I said. "Much less put another one in."

"What Molly described is correct," Vern said. "In modern, mechanized fortune-cookie bakeries. But the old-fashioned way is by hand. It so happens my mother has a friend who was a fortune-cookie editor, and if a batch of cookies was known to have fortunes that were for some reason improper or incorrect, they'd have to change them. You have to remember, in some countries there's government censorship, and the fortune cookie bakers could get into serious trouble if they sent out fortunes critical of officials or contradictory to policy."

Crazy in Poughkeepsie

"Why don't they just throw the whole batch away?"

"You don't know much about business and the way things are done," Vern said. "Now, this is how we remove the old fortune. My mother's friend showed me. It's a knack. Watch me, and remember it's all in the wrist."

Vern took a cookie and shook it with a rotating, snapping motion. Sure enough, a tiny corner of the white slip of paper appeared from the thin line of separation every fortune cookie has. Vern grabbed the tiny corner with his fingernails, pulled out the slip of paper, put the now-fortuneless fortune cookie aside, and picked up another one. "Give it a try. It's easy once you get just the right wrist-snap."

It took hours. Once we had de-fortuned the large number of cookies, we had to slip the new bits of paper into them, which was actually harder than shaking out the old ones.

"I'll just pop around to the Sha Dan Duang Palace and slip this bag back into place," Vern said. "Be back in a few." Vern scurried up the basement steps and was gone.

"And he thinks I'm the crazy one," Molly said. "Which, of course, I am, but he is not a scintilla less crazy than me. Of course, I agree with and admire his environmental concern, but he just got us to spend hours switching fortunes in cookies, and that includes you, so who isn't crazy in our little group? And don't say the dog is crazy. She gets a pass because she's a good pupster. Aren't you a good pupster, Lhasa, dear?"

"I'm saying nothing," I said.

"I wouldn't be surprised if orangutans are being forced to work in that fortune cookie bakery."

18.

"I wonder what happened with the Guru, and where is he?"

"I got a postcard from him," Vern Chuckoff said.

"When was this?"

"Just today. I was going to mention it, but I forgot."

"But you remembered to get us to wake up early and help you launch two hundred balloons carrying little notes that say, 'Ground-level ozone gonna getcha.' So what does the postcard say?"

"He says he's having a nice time, hopes we are all well, he'll be back soon, and he wants us to go to Tod Town and look at some circus wagons."

Daniel Pinkwater

"Tod Town? What's that? Also, what exactly is a circus wagon?"

"Tod Town is a neighborhood," Molly said. "I've been there, and a circus wagon is obviously a wagon that has something to do with a circus."

"Ever seen one, personally?"

"No, have you?"

It was surprising—actually it was amazing—that Molly knew about a neighborhood Vern Chuckoff, who had lived in Poughkeepsie all his life, had never heard of. I, too, had never heard of it, and besides having lived in Poughkeepsie all my life, I had taken lots of walks with the Guru that covered the town street by street and block by block, like looking for a needle in a haystack. Molly had, until recently, lived in some little village up in the Catskills, with no telephone, no internet, no electricity, and yet she knew about it. What was more, it sounded like an interesting neighborhood . . . in Poughkeepsie!

"It was started by a famous movie director, way back in history," Molly said. "There used to be a lot of circus folks and what they used to call 'living attractions' who made homes there

82

Crazy in Poughkeepsie

I guess it makes sense that there might be some circus wagons around."

"How can you possibly know stuff like this?"

"You think I'm ignorant because I'm a hick from the backwoods," Molly said. "The fact is, I'm practically a genius when it comes to knowing things."

The first interesting thing about this neighborhood was that it was not close to any wide forty-five-miles-per-hour commuter roads, or highways with strip malls, parking lots, and discount stores on both sides. I had noticed on my walks with the Guru that the city must have once been a sort-of continuous place, with houses, schools, stores, churches, all having grown up sort of naturally, over hundreds of years. At some point, it had apparently been sliced through by wide roads. Most places in town, you could hear traffic, and ambulances, and fire engines, far away, and not so far, day and night, from left and right.

To get to Tod Town, we made a right off the Samuel Slocum Turnpike, went past some abandoned little factories that looked very old, and turned left at the ruins of the old pin works where they made, and invented, pins—regular

83

straight pins, a big deal at the time. We passed a few old-looking farmhouses, and even a couple of little farms; we saw a horse or two and a couple of cows.

The houses were built closer together, we noticed, as we walked along Hercules Avenue. They were small and old-looking, well-kept, with nice paint jobs, and gardens and pots of flowers. There was a guy sitting in his front yard.

"Hi, kids," the guy said.

He was of unusual appearance.

"Excuse us for a minute, mister," Molly said. "I have to tell something to my friend."

She pulled me out into the middle of the street. "Do not make the remark you were about to make."

"What remark? I was going to make no remark."

"Under your breath, out of the side of your mouth, you were going to comment on that guy."

"What? The guy sitting in his front yard? The guy who looks like . . ."

"Stop right there. You were going to say something about the way he looks."

"Not anything bad. I was just going to remark."

"Belay that remarking, buddy. I've got a feeling we may meet more people who are put together in ways you haven't seen before, so I'll give you a thirty-second course in etiquette. When you encounter someone physically radical, do not speak about that person as if they were not present, whisper to who you're with, or make faces or gestures. You can speak to the person, because it's a person, and if you don't mind the risk of seeming a little boorish you can go straight to making reference to how they look and how they got that way, they're used to it. Mostly it's good manners not to bring it up until they do."

"Thanks," I said. "I was just surprised, is all."

"Where I come from, the males are all, like, four foot seven, with beards right down to their navels, little button eyes, and noses like Idaho potatoes. Just a matter of luck that the females are all good-looking like me, but we learn not to remark when people are surprising-looking."

"OK, I have been advised."

"This goes for you, too, Vern. Back home, the boys wouldn't even go into town because the so-called normal people couldn't get over anyone looking a little different. It gets tedious."

"Hi back atcha, citizen," Molly said to the guy in his front yard. "What's to do around here?"

"Here in the neighborhood?" the guy said. "The big draw is the Gooble Gobble Country Kitchen. People go there for the jitterbugs."

The Gooble Gobble Country Kitchen was a sort of fancied-up shack a few yards along the street. There was a sign on it: WE GOT JITTER-BUGS.

"So what is a jitterbug?" Molly asked.

"It's the National Dish of Poughkeepsie," I said. "It's a slice of meatloaf or a hamburger on top of a piece of white bread with a scoop of mashed potatoes on top of that and brown gravy all over."

"That sounds fairly disgusting," Molly said.

"It is. But it's traditional."

As we walked along, we saw several people of extremely unusual appearance. I was glad that Molly had spoken to me. I knew how to behave.

"So, who's for a jitterbug?" Molly asked.

"I'll just watch," I said.

"Me too," Vern said.

"We have to order something if we're going in," Molly said.

"Toast for me," I said.

"Yes, toast," Vern said.

"Why are we even going inside?" I asked.

"Talk to the locals," Vern said. "We're looking for a blue circus wagon."

"A blue one?"

"Yes."

"Do you have that postcard with you?" Vern gave me the postcard. I read it. "Yep, he wants us to find a blue circus wagon, and get it cleaned up and ready to roll. Vern, why didn't you tell us the whole postcard?"

"I've got global warming to think about. I can't get caught up in details."

19.

Stepping inside the Gooble Gobble Country Kitchen was a unique experience. It was fairly busy, and the appearance of about half the people in the place would have surprised me a few minutes earlier. In fact, I had become accustomed to the physically unusual in a remarkably short time, and what I noticed first about the people in the restaurant was that they seemed friendly and nice. Molly, of course, was completely comfortable with them, and everybody spoke freely to her, as though they already knew her.

"I'm not going to be able to finish my jitterbug," Molly said. "Either of you guys want some?"

"I'm good with my toast," I said.

"Mmm, toast! Yummy!" Vern Chuckoff said.

A neighborhoodnik named George had joined us at our table. It was impressive to see him deal with pancakes and syrup using his toes.

"How about you, George? Want jitterbug?"

"That stuff's for tourists," George said. "I'm more of a pancake man. Now, to your question about a blue circus wagon, I'm not sure, but if anyone around here has one, it would be Valter van der Seagull."

"Walter?"

"Valter."

"Seagull? Like the bird?"

"It's his name. Valter van der Seagull. I don't know if it has anything to do with the bird. You can ask him yourself when you go to find out about the blue circus wagon."

Crazy in Poughkeepsie

"Vhere . . . I mean where . . . does Valter van der Seagull hang out?"

George gestured over his shoulder with his toe. "You can go across the field behind the Gooble Gobble, and you'll come to a little dirt road. Make a right, and you'll come to his place in about a minute. Little house, five big barns. Lots of people call him Valter Five Barns."

"Because he has five barns."

"No, that's just a coincidence. He came from a town in Connecticut called Five Barns."

"Because there are five barns there."

"I suppose so. I've never been."

20.

"What you got there, sonny? Is that a ghost-flute?" Valter van der Seagull was a round little man in overalls. He was the roundest person I had ever seen.

"I guess so," I said.

"Can you play it?"

"I can hardly get it to make a sound."

"Stick around. There's going to be a bombinating circle in a little while. Bring the flute."

"Bombinating circle?"

"We have one every day."

In a field, between Valter van der Seagull's neat little farmhouse and his five barns, there were several caravans parked in a group. They were like old-timey horse-drawn trailers, or little houses on wheels. Some of them had smoke coming from chimneys, and there were women in wide skirts doing washing, chopping wood, and working in little vegetable patches, and men with big hats and big moustaches, sitting around smoking big pipes.

"Over there, that's where we'll bombinate," Valter van der Seagull said. "Afterwards we'll look at wagons," and he wandered away.

"Bombinate? What's 'bombinate'?" I asked nobody in particular.

"I think I know," Molly said.

"Tell."

"Later. Let's see if I'm right. I see people gathering around that big tree. Let's go over and join them."

21.

"Bombinate" means to hum, or make a humming noise. The people spread out around a great big beech tree that looked like it must have been hundreds of years old. They just stood there, with their eyes closed. Vern Chuckoff and Molly from across the river were not far away. I didn't know why, but I closed my eyes too. Then I became aware that I had been gently rocking from foot to foot for some minutes. Someone began humming, softly, then someone else. It wasn't like they were humming a song, just humming; I felt the vibrations. Some of the vibrations were bouncing against me, and some of the vibrations were coming from inside me. I was rocking

and turning left and right, it wasn't a dance, but it was dancy.

Without meaning to, or thinking about it, almost not aware I was doing it, I lifted the flute to my lips and blew into it. It made a sound! Not only did it make a sound, it was a nice sound, and it matched with all the bombinating that was going on all around me. For a second, or less than a second, I wondered if Vern and Molly were bombinating, too, but I was so busy humming and at the same time blowing notes out of my flute, and rocking and turning in a dancy way, that I never bothered to just open my eyes and take a look. Then my fingertips got themselves lined up with the finger holes in the flute, and my fingers—not me but my fingers— knew when to press down and cover a hole and when to lift up and open a hole, so the flute could play scales and notes and tunes.

Then the bombination stopped. Just stopped. Nothing sudden, and no gradually coming in for a landing. It just naturally came to an end, and instead of the humming, which had been so nice, there was silence, and that was just as nice. Some of the people sat down on the ground and took a little rest, others just walked away, some of them shook hands or hugged other bombinators.

Lhasa, the Guru's Kali dog, woke up and shook herself. She'd slept peacefully through the whole humming.

I asked Molly, "Is this what you thought it would be?"

"More or less," she said. "We used to do this in my village in the mountains. It was pretty much the same, only we never had a flute player. Nice work, by the way. I thought you said you couldn't play it."

"I'm taking lessons." I said.

22.

Valter van der Seagull was by far the roundest person I had ever seen. I wondered if his overalls were specially made round ones. He also had round little hands and round little feet, round eyes and a round nose. To top it off, literally, he was wearing a sort of round hat.

"What's your name?" he asked me.

"Mick."

"So, where'd you get the ghost flute, Mick?"

"An old guy, he's a guru, gave it to me. I think he got it from some ghosts, or in a place where ghosts were hanging out."

"A guru, you say. It wouldn't be the guru who wanders the streets of Poughkeepsie with a kid and a dog?"

"That's him. His name is Guru Lumpo Smythe-Finkel, and I'm the kid who wanders with him. I guess I'm sort of his pupil. Anyway, he was the one who gave me this flute. He said I should learn to play it."

"I've seen that guru," Valter van der Seagull said. "He's bombinated with us a couple of times. It's a rare and special thing, that flute. As I understand it, you don't so much learn to play it as get so you can play it. Happens automatic. But what do I know? I'm an old circus guy, not a psychiatrist."

"Why would you need to be a psychiatrist to know about ghost flutes?"

"Exactly. You were asking about a blue circus wagon, were you not?"

"You have such a wagon?"

"I have a bunch of good old wagons, but most of them done broke down. However, the blue one is all right, just needs a heck of a cleanup."

"Can we see the wagon?" Molly asked.

"You can see it when I take you where it is," Valter van der Seagull said. "You can't see it from here."

"Will you take us to where the wagon is?"

"Bless your heart, of course I will. What sort

of wagon psychiatrist would I be if I didn't let you see my wagon?"

"Are you a wagon psychiatrist?"

"Of course not. There's no such thing. Let's go over to the barn, and you can see the wagon."

"Do you think this guy is crazy?" I whispered to Vern Chuckoff.

"It's possible. He mentions psychiatrists a lot. Maybe he needs to see one."

Valter van der Seagull was walking our little group in the direction of his barns. A little old woman with a rag wrapped around her head, and earrings, grabbed Vern by the arm with her bony old hand. "Eet is not your fawlt, my

son," she said. "You vere born under an unlucky star."

"I beg your pardon?" Vern said.

"The volf! The volf that bit you! Eet is not your fawlt."

"What volf . . . I mean wolf? I was never bitten by a wolf. I've never even seen a wolf."

"Oh! I apologize. I mistook you for someone else. But the thing about the unlucky star still goes." The old woman hurried away.

"That's old Maria," Valter van der Seagull said. "She means well. Pay her no mind. And, let me be the first to say, I'm sorry to hear about the unlucky star, young man."

"What unlucky star? I don't believe in stuff like that," Vern Chuckoff said.

"Quite right. You're a scientist," Molly said. Then she winked at me and whispered, "He's doomed. I saw the mark of the werewolf on him first time we ever met."

23.

It was a pretty big barn Valter van der Seagull
took us to. We had to help him swing the
wide and high double doors open. Valter flipped
a switch, and a whole bunch of light fixtures
came on. The place was huge, cavernous, and
full of amazing wagons. They were big and old-
fashioned-looking, and called "wagons" only
because there was nothing else to call them.
They were more like boxcars, or those houses on
wheels we had seen outside than something I'd
have pictured being called a wagon. Some of
them were works of art, with fancy paint jobs,
and carved decorations of flowers, and cupids,
and curlicues; others had circus posters and
advertisements for various shows: Cheifetz
Brothers' Circus, Von Fenster's Wild West Show,

Crazy in Poughkeepsie

and Laughran's Trained Sloths. Some wagons had bars, like a cage, along the sides, to carry lions and tigers, and show them off.

"Wow!" I said.

"Wow!" Vern Chuckoff said.

"What were these things used for?" Molly asked Valter van der Seagull.

"Century before last," Valter van der Seagull said, "most Americans lived in small towns in rural areas. These towns were too small to have anything like a theater, and of course things like movies, let alone radio and television, hadn't been invented yet. There wasn't much to do in the way of entertainment other than gather in the general store, tell lies, and spit on the hot stove. So entertainment came to the towns. Lacking a place to put on a show, the shows set up a big tent with seats around the inside, and that was the theater. Some people were educated and some people were ignorant, so it made sense to put on shows that everybody could enjoy, unusual animals, acrobats, clowns, music, ladies in fancy costumes standing on one foot on big white horses, guys who'd go into a cage with lions and tigers and get them to do tricks."

"I wouldn't mind seeing a show like that," Molly said.

"Of course you wouldn't. So the big traveling circuses went on into the middle of the twentieth century, and beyond the middle. They didn't just come to small towns. For a long time, the circuses had come to big cities, too. Then they started to die out."

"Why was that? Did audiences prefer movies and television?"

"That may have been part of it, more kinds of competition, and tastes change. It's not that circuses are completely extinct, but pretty nearly so, and I think it all had to do with elephants."

"We need you to explain that."

"Well, circus work was very hard. It was hard for the circus people, and hard for the circus animals. Imagine this: You come to a town early in the morning. You arrive in a long line of trucks, and in earlier times, wagons like the ones we're looking at. You've been driving through the night. The first thing you do is unload the tent and set it up. It's a really big tent, made of heavy canvas in big rolls, and held up by wooden poles as tall as tall trees. The poles have to be set in place and pulled up with ropes; everything is heavy. When the thing is done, it's big enough for a performing space in the middle, and bleacher seats for maybe a thousand people all around the inside. So every circus had some strong guys to do this kind of work, but most of it was done by the elephants."

"The elephants did it?"

"Elephants are really smart and incredibly strong. One elephant, working with just one guy whose job is just to walk alongside and sort of watch, can put up a whole pretty large circus tent all by itself, and two or three elephants working together can put up a monstrous huge one. Now, these elephants have been riding all night, and they're going to do routines in the show come evening that involve dancing and doing handstands, and all kinds of tricks. Then, let's say it's a small town with only enough audience for one performance, they're going to strike the tent and put it on trucks that very night, climb into their own wagons, sleep standing up, and do the same thing the next morning."

"That's pretty amazing."

"Elephants are amazing animals. But you

have to admit, what I'm describing is the hardest kind of work. The circus people work hard, too. They work as hard, the humans, as the elephants do, as elephants, but there's a difference. Know what it is?"

"The people have a choice," Vern Chuckoff said.

"Exactly. Some circus people have argued that the elephants enjoy working, and there is some reason to believe this is true, but there's no way to ask them. Even in countries where elephants are used to doing hard work, such as helping to harvest and move big heavy trees, they get to take a bath in a river, sleep outdoors, take a break between doing heavy stuff, and just hang out being elephants. So some people who cared about animal welfare, and some of them were circus people, started to be concerned that circus work was an unfair deal for the animals, starting with the elephants."

"I get it," Vern Chuckoff said. "I completely get it. For maybe hundreds of years, elephants traveled with circuses, entertained in the shows, and doubled as tractors, and nobody gave any thought to whether it was fair or not. Then, as I have been explaining to my friends here, once an idea starts to move around, it goes everywhere. So seemingly all of a sudden, people stopped feeling good about elephants, and other animals working in circuses."

"So one by one, circuses stopped having animal acts. There are still some traveling circuses, with acrobats and clowns, but without the elephants," said Valter van der Seagull.

"Do you think the elephants miss working in the circus?" Molly asked.

"If you go to the Bronx Zoo in New York City, there are a couple of retired circus elephants there, and every so often they will do their old dance routine for the people. I think they enjoyed their circus days. I can't say if they miss them. There are a couple of places where the circus stays in one place and people go to it, and the animals have decent working conditions, which is good, but the traveling circus just isn't a big deal anymore.

"And speaking of elephants, you told me you were interested in a blue wagon. I only have one that's blue, and it was used to transport elephants. At one time it belonged to Captain Bobby Gibbs, a great elephant man. A half dozen pachyderms could ride in it"

24.

It was the biggest wagon in the place, and a beautiful blue color, with white carved doodads all over it. It was a little beaten up, but not too bad.

"So you're interested in this wagon?" Valter asked. "May I know what you propose to do with it?"

"Well, we're instructed."

"Instructed?"

"By the Guru. He says to get it cleaned up and ready to roll."

"That's doable. Were you planning to buy it or rent it?"

"What's the rent?" Molly asked.

"Thousand a month."

"Can we rent it for less than a month?"

"Nope."

"How much to buy it?"

"Thousand."

"Same as renting it?"

"This wagon doesn't move for less than a grand, which happens to be the amount I owe for electricity, fuel, water, and taxes. So, what do you say?"

"I say sold," Molly said.

What? Wait a second! Molly told Valter van der Seagull we'd buy the wagon for a thousand bucks?

"But we don't have a thousand dollars," I said.

"Sure we do," Molly said. "I have access to unlimited money. I've told you that before, but you chose to assume I'm untruthful just because I'm crazy and sleep in a tree." To Valter van der Seagull she said, "Let's step outside for a moment. I want to discuss a detail or two of the transaction with you in private."

Molly from across the river and Valter van der Seagull went out of the barn, and far enough away that Vern Chuckoff and I could not hear what they were saying. When they returned, Valter's manner had changed. It wasn't that he hadn't been friendly enough before, but now it seemed as though he was very impressed with us, especially Molly.

"I can lend you brooms and brushes and shovels," Valter said. "And of course, I'll help you with the work. The wagon hasn't been used for transporting elephants for a long time, but there have been horses, pigs, chickens, and tons of hay, so there's all kinds of schmootz to clear out. I will get underneath and make sure everything is greased, and the tires have air in them. And I want to say, it's an honor to have dealings with you."

"What's with him?" I whispered to Molly.

"He's heard of my family."

"What are they, the mafia?"

"Lots older than that, and very nice, too, but people have the idea that it's a bad thing to get them mad at you. Pure superstition, of course."

"So, are you going to pay him a thousand for the wagon?"

"I gave him a coin. He's happy with it."

"You gave him a coin? For a thousand dollar wagon, you gave him a coin?"

"It's gold. He got a good deal."

"Who are you, anyway?" I asked Molly. "And who's your family?"

"I'll tell you all about it sometime. More to the point, why did the Guru tell us to get this wagon, and get it ready, why and for what?"

25.

When I got home after my second full day of cleaning schmootz out of the big blue circus wagon, the Guru was sitting cross-legged on his bed in my room. Lhasa was overjoyed to see him. He dug into a crumpled white paper bag, pulled out a ring-shaped pastry, and broke off a piece.

"For my good girl," he said. "And some Wisconsin kringle, for you too, Mick." He handed me a chunk. I took a bite. It wasn't bad.

"So what happened with the wagon?" the Guru asked me.

"Valter, he's the guy with all the wagons, wanted a thousand dollars for it. Molly paid him off with a coin, and then he went all obsequious. Do you know what that was about?"

"She's
a VanDwerg.
They have a secret gold
mine up in the mountains. They're
sort of like the good folk."

"The good folk?"

"It's considered bad luck to say the word, but
it rhymes with schmeprekon, get it?"

"Lepre—"

"Don't say it. Though Molly's crowd isn't exactly the same thing, best to respect tradition.
So, I expect there was a lot of schmootz to
clear out."

"We just finished up today, but none of us
has any idea why you wanted us to get the
thing. Also where have you been and what's
going on in general?"

"I've been all over, making inquiries. Want some more Wisconsin kringle?"

"You were in Wisconsin?"

"All over. As to what's going on, you'll find out tonight. Tell the other kids to show up in the parking lot of the old butter churn factory a little before midnight. I'll brush the dog, and you get cleaned up and put on some nice clothes— you're going to a party."

26.

I do not have a lot of experience with parties, almost none, in fact, if you don't count little kids' birthday parties with the paper hats and the cake and ice cream. This means I don't personally have a basis for comparison, but I feel safe in saying that a party with ghosts is completely unlike any other party anyone may have been to. For one thing, ghosts are immaterial, as everyone knows. This means that a whole lot of ghosts can fit in a given space, even a small space, but this was a big space, and the number of ghosts was beyond counting. Also, as everyone also knows, ghosts are formerly alive people. . . . There have been a lot of people who were formerly alive and are now ghostly, and these ghosts will naturally include individuals with any number of skills and talents. Take music, for example. At this party there was a hot ghost band, Tuba Spooky, and they were good. "Hot" is a figure of speech—ghosts don't have a temperature.

Of course, ghosts are light on their feet. It would be better to say they are weightless on their feet. I had never heard anything about ghosts liking to dance, but these ghosts did. I danced, too. I danced with a number of ghosts, one at a time and in bunches. I can't possibly say I was able to keep up with them, but I got into the dancing, and I think I gave a pretty good account of myself, for a living person. Ghosts do not get all sweaty and disheveled when they dance a lot, and they don't get out of breath and have to take a rest. As at any well-organized party, there were snacks and drinks. Only ghosts don't eat. However, they like to sniff things, so there was a table with the most delicious-looking pizzas, pizzas of every description with every possible—and some impossible—toppings. The fragrance was divine . . . only . . . this is something I submit almost nobody who hasn't partied with the deceased knows . . . it was ghostly pizza! It was immaterial, it was weightless, if you went to take a slice, your fingers closed on each other! Molly from across the river, who turned out to be something of a pizza expert, said if it had been of this world, it would be the best pizza in the history of ever. To drink, which is to say sniff in lieu of drinking, there were cups of fleegix, which is what I would have expected at a ghostly party, only of course this fleegix was immaterial and without worldly existence.

So this was the party. Good music. The ghosts were pleasant and friendly. The female ghosts were pretty and the male ghosts were handsome, and all of them were great dancers. There was great-smelling pizza, which drove me a little crazy. (The Guru told me we'd all stop and get an eatable slice at the Dawn Patrol 24-Hour Pizzeria on the way home.) All in all, it was the best party I'd ever been to, or was likely to experience until maybe after my death. But all that wasn't the best thing. It was all good stuff, and I wouldn't have missed it for anything, but there was something much bigger than all the goings-on, and by much bigger, I mean much, much bigger. And that something was Luna.

Luna, of course, was the lovable whale who'd

been described to those of us who hadn't met her, namely Vern Chuckoff and myself. When we met her, the description fell far short of what she was. She was lovable all right, in a whale-size way. It wasn't her looks, though she was a particularly attractive ghost whale. And it wasn't her manner. She was sweet and charming, and looked at me with one very beautiful whale eye at a time, but it wasn't that. It wasn't her grace, though she was one of the best dancers at the party. And it wasn't her conversation, because she said not a word. It was something else. Waves of sweetness radiated off her like road shimmer, heat haze, rising from the pavement on a hot summer day. I don't remember the first time I ever tasted ice cream, but I have seen infants react to it. Being near Luna was like that.

27.

I wasn't the only one to fall in love with Luna. The Guru, Molly, Vern Chuckoff, and I talked about her when we stopped at the Dawn Patrol 24-Hour Pizzeria after we left the party, which was in full swing when we went out the door.

"Some whale, wouldn't you say?" the Guru asked.

"She's a peach, all right," Molly said.

"I feel that I'm a better person because I met her," I said.

"What is this cassava-leaf pizza?" Vern Chuckoff asked.

"The pizza man, Milton Kamara, is from Africa," the Guru said. "Cassava leaves are a big favorite there."

"From Sierra Leone?" Molly asked.

"How did you know?"

"Strange to say, I know another pizza man from Sierra Leone," Molly said.

"World culture," Vern Chuckoff said.

"I'll have to ask Milton if he knows my pizza guy," Molly said.

Milton overheard her. "Arnold Babatunji? He is my cousin."

"I bet half the people in Sierra Leone are your cousins."

"Pretty near."

"So, we're all agreed, Luna is a special whale," the Guru said.

"Oh, more than special."

"Super special."

"She's the whale of whales."

"Would you all be prepared to go out of your way to do something for her?"

"Of course, but what could some kids and a guru do for a ghostly whale?"

"There is something. First, I don't suppose any of you has a driver's license. No? We'll have to get your brother, Maurice, to help us with the driving."

"What driving?"

"There's driving to be done. We're all going on a road trip. We'll be gone for some time."

"What do you call some time?"

"Days, weeks, months, maybe. We won't know until we know."

"Well, that is OK for Molly. She has no fixed address, sleeps in trees, and does not attend school, as far as I know, but school will be starting soon for Vern and me. Plus, our parents might not want us to go off for days, weeks, or months."

"I've already spoken to your parents. They agree that traveling with a guru would be an educational opportunity."

"What about school?"

"I sent notes to your teachers. You're both excused."

"Excused? Why would they excuse us based on a note from some guru?"

"I signed the note as 'Superintendent of Schools.'"

"But you're not Superintendent of Schools."

"I am. Superintendent of Schools, Kalimpong, West Bengal. It's an honorary title."

"You left out the part about Kalimpong, West Bengal, didn't you?"

124

Crazy in Poughkeepsie

"I don't remember. I was in a hurry."

I had been starting to put two and two together. "You need Maurice to drive, because we're going to tow the blue circus wagon somewhere, and Luna, the ghostly whale, is going to ride in the wagon."

"Bingo! Bull's-eye! You have it exactly!"

"And we're taking the ghost whale on a trip that may go on for weeks or months."

"Or days or hours. One doesn't know. But probably not years, or even a year."

"Ghosts, even whale ghosts, are immaterial and weightless. Why do we need to schlep Luna in the big circus wagon?"

"What would you have us do, buy her a ticket for the bus?"

"I sort of see your point, sort of, your sort of point. But, in your usual inscrutable fashion, you're not going to tell us what this is all about, where we're going, what we hope to find, and that sort of thing."

"On the contrary, I will tell you the whole megillah this instant."

28.

We settled down cross-legged on the little bit of lawn outside the Dawn Patrol 24-Hour Pizzeria, nibbling our cassava-leaf slices, and the Guru explained. "The natural history of whales is very interesting. It's hard to believe, but the largest animal on the planet, and a fully aquatic one, is the descendant of a quite small, even-toed ungulate that resided in the Himalayas."

"What's an ungulate?" Vern Chuckoff wanted to know.

"I'm not sure. I think it may be some kind of bunny. Anyway, this bunny, or ungulate, evolved into something else, and that something evolved into something else again, and that which had evolved some more. I'm pretty sure there's something about this in the Vedas, which are part of the Hindu scriptures, or maybe it's in the Upanishads, but I, personally, have never run across it.

"Anyway, at one point in the evolutionary sequence starting with the cute little bunny in the Himalayas, one of the evolved examples dipped a toe in water, and then a few million years later, another generation took a little swim. In no time at all, which is to say fifty million years, a creature along the line of descent existed that was fully aquatic. Also, it had developed a streamlined body, similar to a fish, and was all ready to turn into the modern whale that we know and love.

"I have left the serious and technical science out of this explanation in order to get to the important bit, and also because it is hard, but the only thing you need to remember is that whales started out as a terrestrial animal and evolved into an aquatic one. Although they are mammals and warm-blooded, and breathe air, they can't live outside the sea. For one thing, they evolved into something so large and heavy that they need the water to support them. If they were on land for an appreciable time, their weight would squash their organs and they would be unable to live.

"Now, as you have seen, a ghostly whale has no trouble like that. Dear Luna doesn't need to be in water in order to be comfortable, weightless and immaterial as she is. She can even dance, and dance very charmingly, I'm sure you agree.

"I've been telling you about the natural history of whales as regards their physical being, but as with every creature, there's more to them than the physical. There's personal, and cultural, and spiritual. Scientists haven't gone very far into what whales think, let alone what they feel and believe, but at least one guru has."

"Let me guess," Molly said. "You are that guru."

"Well, no, I am not. It's a guru named Swami Talmy. I've spoken with him and read his book about cognitive cetology—cetology being the study of whales. He can understand what the creatures are saying, and here's the thing I'm explaining my way up to . . . Whales like being aquatic, they like spending their lives in the sea, they like to swim and dive, eat fish or plankton, depending on what kind of whales they are. They like to leap out of the water and smack the surface with their flukes—that's 'tails' to you. In general, whales have a lot of fun . . . while they are alive. But, in their ancient myths and legends, which go back millions of years, there is a belief that when they die, they go to a whalish heaven, and it's not ocean at all. It's on land. Oh, it's a beautiful place with meadows and flowers and grass, it's a kind of Whaleysian Fields or Whalhalla. There, the spirits of all the whales that ever were can romp and gambol and play in the sunshine. And, get this, it's a real place."

"Only nobody knows where it is," I said.

"Right," the Guru said.

"And Luna wants to go there," Vern Chuckoff said.

"Right again."

"And we're going to find it! We're going to take her there!" Molly said.

"You kids are so smart!" the Guru said.

29.

"But I have classes!" Maurice said. "You want me to drive somewhere, and you don't know where that somewhere is, and I'm supposed to tow a circus wagon with the ghost of a whale in it?"

"That's about the size of it."

"I'm not going to do it."

"You owe me. You took me from my established life in the Himalayas, and brought me to Poughkeepsie, not to mention you did the same thing to my dog, Lhasa."

"You were living in a cave, and you were behind on your rent, which I paid for you. The dog was living on roadside scallions, and didn't dream of getting factory fresh kibble every day, plus scrambled eggs, and doughnuts, and whatever else you've been giving her. And you have an actual bed in my own brother's room, and free access to my comic collection. I don't see that I owe you so much, plus I have an exam coming."

"I know your professor," the Guru said. "I'll fix it for you."

"You know my professor? Professor Tag, who teaches cognitive accountancy?"

"Mick knows him too. So does the dog. We've stopped by his house a couple of times. They gave us very nice corn muffins on both occasions. I'm sure he'll give you a pass."

Vern Chuckoff and Molly from across the river were impressed when they saw the Buick. It was huge and powerful looking, obviously able to tow a circus wagon with ease, and our grandfather had caused a shiny trailer hitch to be installed. Maurice, his father before him, and his grandfather before that, had lovingly waxed and polished the car so the chrome, of which there was a lot, sparkled and shone. The paint was glossy black, and it had big fat whitewall tires. The Guru had stocked the car with plenty of snacks, bags of kibble, and a large cooler, apparently an official accessory, with BUICK in silver letters. It was full of orange soda. You pushed a button and the soda came out of a little spigot.

It was just a matter of driving out to Tod Town to pick up the wagon from Valter van der Seagull, and then to the old churnworks to get Luna. Maurice had never met Luna, and of course he fell in love with her, and that was the end of his moaning and complaining about missing his classes at community college and his low-level kibbling job so he could go on a mystical trip with a ghost of a whale, a guru, and us kids.

Transferring Luna to the wagon had to be done at night, not that we were doing anything wrong and did not have a perfect right to put a whale ghost in a wagon, but it would have attracted attention, and caused a lot of comment. It was easily done. She just floated out of the abandoned factory and settled into the wagon as nicely as you please. We had put a lot of cushions and fuzzy blankets and taped-up pictures cut out of magazines inside the wagon to make it more comfy and homelike, not that Luna noodod that stuff, and I'm sure she didn't care, but we just loved her so much, we needed to do it.

We were all in love with Luna, but the one most in love was Lhasa, the Tibetan Kali dog, and it was mutual. We all took turns riding in the wagon with the whale, but Lhasa rode with her all the time.

"Everybody ready?" Guru Lumpo Smythe-Finkel asked. "Got your seat belts on? Anybody need to use the bathroom? Remember, do not operate the toaster while the car is in motion." Grandfather had purchased every possible option, and the car had a built-in toaster. "OK, Maurice, drive!"

"Where do I drive to, or toward what?" Maurice asked the Guru.

"Just drive. Let's get started."

"You don't know where we're going, do you?"

"Of course I know. We're going to the place where the spirits of the whales go."

"But you don't know where it's located."

"I give you that, but I do know how to get there."

"We'd all like to know what you know about knowing how to get there. Would you care to expand a little?"

"Of course. It's perfectly simple. Just start driving."

"And then what do we do?"

"Never be afraid to ask directions."

30.

"So, we just pull into a gas station, or stick our heads out the window and ask some local walking along the roadside, 'Hey! Do you know how to get to the place whales go when they die?'"

"We can do that," the Guru said. "But I doubt we'll get much useful information."

"So, of whom do we ask directions?"

"Me, of course. I don't know why everybody keeps forgetting they're traveling with a qualified guru."

"So you do have some idea of where we're supposed to be going."

"Not a one, but if you suddenly ask me, 'Where do we go now?' there's a good chance I'll suddenly shout out, 'Turn left at the next intersection,' or something equally directiony. That's if I'm inspired in the moment."

"Shouldn't we consult the global positioning thingie?" Vern Chuckoff asked.

"We don't have one," Maurice said. "This car is pre-digital, but there's a blue light that comes on when we are on the Interstate."

"The Interstate Highway System, which was just being completed when this car was built?" Vern asked.

"I think it's more likely to be the system of virtual or quasi-imaginary roads or routes that exists in between the state of so-called reality in which we operate and some other states of existence of which we are ordinarily unaware," Molly said.

"How does a mere slip of a girl from a Dwergish village in the mountains know about that?" the Guru wanted to know.

"Book I found in the Kingston High School library," Molly said. "The story is strangely similar to what's happening with us now."

"Well, you know, some people believe there are a finite number of possible plots," the Guru said. "In addition to sometimes responding to queries as to direction, the driver   that's you,

ALTERNATE
ROUTE

Maurice . . . should be prepared for me to suddenly shout out something like . . ." And then he shouted, "Turn right! Do it quickly, or we'll have to go all around the block."

Maurice managed to make the right turn without crashing the car. We were on the approach to the bridge across the Hudson River, and then we were on it.

"Here comes Route 9W," the Guru said. "I know a joke about that road. It goes like this: 'What question is answered with the answer "9W"?' The question is 'Does your name begin with a "V" Mr. Wagner?' and the answer is 'Nein, "W."' Ever hear that one before?"

"Yes," said Maurice, Vern, Molly, and me.

We heard a howling.

"Of course! Lhasa!" the Guru said. "She's alerting us. She's tight with the whale, and besides, she's such a smart dog. Look! The sign says, 'ALTERNATE ROUTE!' What could be plainer? Make a left, Maurice."

"Do you think 'Alternate Route' is the same as 'Interstate?'" I asked Molly, who had read the book.

"I wouldn't be surprised," Molly said.

31.

"So, Guru, when you disappeared suddenly, and were gone for some time, communicating by postcards sent to Vern here, where were you all that time?"

"I was all over. Cincinnati, Des Moines, Atlanta, San Diego, the entire state of Kansas, and Sheboygan, Wisconsin."

"And may I ask what you were doing in all those places?"

"I was gathering information."

"About the place where the spirits of whales wind up? The place we're taking Luna?"

"Basically."

"So you know where it is?"

"Nope."

"You don't know?"

"I haven't a clue."

"And yet we are in this car, pulling the enormous circus wagon, and we're supposed to get there."

"Of course."

"With you not knowing where it is."

"I know how to get there."

"Tell me if I get this right. The way to get there is just to drive along without any kind of plan, taking various turns on the spur of the moment."

"With the right attitude."

"And the right attitude is . . ."

"Assuming we'll arrive."

"That's it?"

"That's it."

"Does this kind of approach apply to anything other than seeking a physical location, which is the afterlife for gigantic aquatic mammals?"

"It applies to everything."

"So, how do you think we're doing so far?"

"It couldn't be better. But now we should find a place to camp for the night. And, as a demonstration of the principle I just explained to you, look at the sign."

Crazy in Poughkeepsie

There was a sign:

FIVE MILES TO ROMANY BILL'S DELUXE RESORT, CAMPGROUND, HOBO JUNGLE, AND JUNKYARD.

32.

"I'm pretty sure this place was mentioned in that book I read," Molly said.

There were plenty of sleeping bags, blankets, and pots and pans in the trunk of the Buick, so this was just the sort of place we needed. We pulled into Romany Bill's Deluxe Resort, Campground, Hobo Jungle, and Junkyard.

"Let's look for a secluded campsite," the Guru said. "We'll get a fire started, and then it's roasted potatoes all 'round."

"What do we have besides potatoes?" Molly asked.

"Orange soda," the Guru said. "Little bit of a foul-up in the catering department, but roasted potatoes covered with wood ash is a camping delicacy."

Crazy in Poughkeepsie

Here came Romany Bill himself, wearing three hats. "Welcome to Romany Bill's," he said. "May I offer you the *spécialité de la maison*, cornmeal mush with Mexican peppers? How does that sound to you?"

"Horrible, but better than a potato covered with ashes," Molly said.

"You'll love it," Romany Bill said. "And there's homemade root beer you'll never forget. Do my eyes deceive me, or is that Captain Bobby Gibbs's wagon? The captain isn't among you, by any chance?"

"Afraid not. We got it from a wagon dealer in Poughkeepsie."

"What do you have on board? Elephants?"

"It's a whale."

"No fooling? May I have a look?"

"I have to warn you, this whale is not the usual kind. You have a problem with ghosts?"

"Are you kidding? Some of my best friends . . ."

"Kids, let's get Luna out of the wagon. She's probably tired of being cooped up."

Romany Bill was impressed when he saw Luna, which was predictable. "What a sweet whale! I'm going to whip up some fish soup to go with the mush. It's as close as I can come to plankton, and she may enjoy a sniff, plus you folks will find it delicious. If you have no objection, I'd like to join you for the meal."

"We'll be honored," the Guru said.

Romany Bill hurried off to his kitchen.

"Nice guy," I said. "We're lucky to have stopped here."

"The whole trip is going to be like this," the Guru said.

It appeared we were the only guests at Romany Bill's that night.

"It's probably busier on the weekends," the Guru said. "But it's nice having the whole place to ourselves. Luna can float around and investigate, and we won't have lots of curious people to deal with."

There was a nice moon, and it was a mild night just cool enough to enjoy a campfire. Soon, a fragrance of fish soup and cornmeal mush with Mexican peppers reached us from Romany Bill's kitchen. It smelled wonderful. We sat on logs placed around the fire, and became hungrier and hungrier.

Romany Bill appeared out of the darkness, with a steaming pot in each hand and a bunch of platters stacked on his head. He put the pots just to the side of our campfire so they would keep warm, and handed around plates and spoons.

"I forgot to mention. It's apricot goo with cream for afters," Romany Bill said.

"Yum," we all said.

33.

After the best meal of my life—I speak only for myself, but the others appeared completely happy as well—we all sat around the fire, cuddling with the ghostly Luna and Lhasa. Maurice had mixed just a bit of apricot goo into Lhasa's kibble, and she was particularly happy. We could not have been cozier or more content.

"It's none of my business," Romany Bill said. "But where are you all headed with dear Luna?"

"Well, you may not have known that whales evolved from a land-based creature."

"An even-toed ungulate that existed in what are now known as the Himalayas," Romany Bill said. "Do not assume because of my simple appearance and humble ways that I am not educated. Next you are going to tell me you're about taking her to the whaley pearly gates."

"You know about that?"

"What am I, a schnook? You learn a lot running a place like this. All kinds of people, and others, come through."

"You don't happen to know where it is, this cetacean nirvana, and how to get there?"

"You don't?"

"Not exactly. We just thought we'd stooge along and come upon it serendipity-like."

"Not to change the subject, but tell me about the dog."

"Lhasa? She's a Tibetan Kali."

"Is that like a collie?"

"Only better."

"So, for example, if someone fell down a well, she would go and bring help."

"Not exactly. First, she would never hang out with anyone stupid enough to fall down a well, and second, she would prevent a person from falling down a well, and third, if someone fell down a well in spite of her best efforts, she would get that person out without having to go for help."

"So she's smart."

"As a couple of whips."

"Knows things."

"Incredible."

"But she doesn't like the whale."

"What are you saying? Just look. She loves the whale. We all love the whale, but the dog really, really loves the whale."

"And the Tibetan Kali, and this Kali in particular, unlike 98.4 percent of all dogs, has no sense of direction at all."

"I thought you said you were educated. Tibetan Kalis are the most directional dogs of all. They have an uncanny sense of . . ."

"Of where things are."

"Yes."

"So while you are wandering stooge-like, with no particular idea where, the dog probably knows precisely."

"I have to confess, it hadn't occurred to me."

"Of course, smart as she is, Lhasa can't come out and just tell you in English."

"And none of us, being humans as we are, have ever learned to speak and understand Dog."

"And you do not have a translator bunny."

"Nor have we ever heard of a translator bunny."

"I have one. I'll bring it to you in the morning."

34.

The translator bunny turned out to be a floppy soft toy with long floppy ears and four floppy paws. There was a noisemaker in the bunny's middle; you could squeeze it, and the bunny would make a honking sound. Lhasa took to it immediately. Later, when we left Romany Bill's, she would position herself in the middle of the front seat of the Buick, between Maurice and the Guru, holding the bunny in her mouth.

Romany Bill gave us a splendid breakfast of cornmeal mush without Mexican peppers. Instead there was maple syrup, and also strawberries. We loaded our sleeping bags into the trunk and Luna into the circus wagon. Lhasa took her place as navigator in the front seat.

Crazy in Poughkeepsie

We pulled out of the deluxe resort, campground, hobo jungle, and junkyard, waving out the windows to Romany Bill, who waved back with his three hats.

Calling it a translator bunny was a bit of an overstatement. It didn't actually translate, it honked. It didn't take long to break the code: "HONK HONK HONK HONK HONK HONK" meant, "yes," or "this is it," or "turn right," or "turn left," or "stop here, I have to pee." "HONK HONK" meant, "no," or, "not of interest," or, "I just like to honk the thing occasionally." Lhasa could have done the same thing, communicating by barking, but she appeared to like using the bunny to communicate with us. I think she may have thought it was simpler and thus easier for us to understand.

HONK HONK HONK HONK HONK HONK
"Are you sure, Lhasa?"
HONK HONK HONK HONK HONK HONK
"Turn right here?"
HONK HONK HONK HONK HONK HONK
"It's hardly a road. It's more of a track."
HONK HONK HONK HONK HONK HONK
"There's grass growing out of it, and it leads
up at a pretty steep angle."
HONK HONK HONK HONK HONK HONK
HONK HONK HONK HONK HONK HONK
"OK, she's the one with the bunny. Maurice,
maybe you should put the car in low gear."

"I'm the one with a driver's license," Maurice said. "I know what to do. Sit tight, hold on.
We're going where the dog honked for us to go."

35.

That first almost-not-a-road Lhasa honked us into driving on was far from the worst one. There were unfinished dirt tracks, cow paths, rocky trails, and sometimes we drove along through ditches barely wider than the 1958 Buick Limited Convertible and the circus wagon, and Maurice would have to get out and measure side to side with a piece of branch to make sure we could get through.

Usually these primitive routes led us to higher and higher elevations. Molly had been riding in the circus wagon with Luna, and on a stop Maurice made for no other reason but to sit among the rocks next to the car and cry, she got out. "I'm just about certain I know where we are," she said.

"You do?"

"We're not far from the miserable village where I grew up," she said. "And if I remember correctly, we could have gotten this far on a well-paved county road."

HONK, Lhasa chomped the bunny.

"There's just a little more rough stuff before we get there," Molly said. "I'd better ride up front, or you're sure to miss it. It will be fun to see what the people make of Luna, and I'm already tasting my mother's cooking. There will be pie."

Molly wasn't kidding when she said we'd be sure to miss the village. Even when we were to all intents and purposes there, and looking at it, we didn't see it.

"It's been this way for hundreds of years," Molly said. "Nobody who isn't us can find the place."

"And who do you mean by 'us'?" the Guru asked.

"We all have the same family name. It's VanDwerg. Old Dutch name. I guess you'd say we're a clan. It's just folklore, but we're the ones who are supposed to have slipped Rip Van Winkle a Mickey Finn that time."

Crazy in Poughkeepsie

We dismounted from the Buick, Luna drifting after us, and followed Molly into the village. It was amazing. We couldn't see it. All we could see was forest and trees, and rocks, and bushes, and then all at once we were in a complete old-fashioned little village, with houses, and streets, and smoke coming out of chimneys, and short people going hither and yon. There was no in-between, no outskirts, no approaching. You were in a forest looking like it had been there for a thousand years, and then you were in the village square, snap! In one second! Snap!

"Home sweet home," Molly said. "My house is up this way. I can smell the pies already."

We were starting to draw a crowd. Molly explained later that the appearance of people from outside the village would be something of a sensation all by itself, but a ghostly whale, and a lovable one at that, was something that would go down in history. Nobody in the village was much over five feet tall, and as Molly had mentioned once, the male VanDwergs were little barrel-shaped guys with bushy beards and little button eyes and large button noses, and the females were on the order of normal humans you might see anywhere, except for the old-fashioned clothes they wore. When I say old-fashioned, I don't mean fairy-tale or history-book old-fashioned, but pictures-of-your-grandparents-when-they-were-in-junior-high-school old-fashioned.

The villagers were welcoming and friendly. We met Molly's mother, Mildred; her father, Woodstock; and her sister, Gertie. I could instantly see why Molly loved them, and why she wanted to get away from this village. They were sweet and kind and lovely, and boring to an amazing degree.

The VanDwergs were bombinating people, and nothing could have stopped them from forming a circle with us in it, and Luna at the center, and tuning up for a big hum. Now, I had only participated in a bombination once, and it was definitely a positive experience, which I can recommend to anyone, but bombinating with a whole village-full of people, plus a ghostly whale, was right off the top of the outstanding-humming chart. One of the things I experienced while humming with the village people was seeing the world through Luna's eyes. I knew everybody loved Luna, but I had never wondered why. Now I knew. It was because she loved everyone and everything with a kind of love that can only be expressed in terms of religion. Religion isn't a major thing with me, and I haven't read all the books of all the religions, but from what I do know, I am reasonably certain there is nothing that could possibly come close to what I picked up about how Luna felt about everything, including me!

"Is Luna God?" I asked the Guru while we were having lunch.

"She sure is," the Guru said. "Which is not to say that any whale, living or dead, isn't God, or that I'm not, and you're not, and this melted goat cheese over roasted veggies is not. It's just that it's particularly obvious in Luna's case."

"The whole thing? Everything is God?"

"Take a Guru's word for it. And how about this bread? It's right out of the oven, and what a crispy crust!"

Molly's clanfolk had pulled long tables into the village square and covered them with platters and bowls of amazing things to eat. There were too many dishes for me to have sampled

157

everything, but there was a corn-and-mushroom soup I will remember as long as I live, and more kinds of pie and cake than anyone can imagine. I also experienced goat cheese in many wonderful forms. It was the lunch of lunches.

We were sitting with Molly's family. "So, tell us about your life in the outside world, dear," Molly's mother, Mildred VanDwerg, said.

"I wound up in Poughkeepsie," Molly said. "And it seems I've lost my mind."

"Well, you know, dear, that will happen," her mother said. "I'm sure it's temporary . . . or it's not. And you have these nice friends."

"Yes, the Guru is an actual guru from New Jersey, and the dog is a Tibetan Kali. The three boys are just boys, but they are very nice."

"And there's the whale."

"Yes, we all love the whale."

Crazy in Poughkeepsie

"Do you have a nice place to live? Do you need any money?"

"I've been sleeping in a tree. I imagine I'll be picked up and thrown into the loony bin by the time the weather turns cold, and I've got about a million dollars in gold."

"You know, you're growing up. I'm not sure it's proper for a girl your age to sleep in a tree."

"I know, mother."

36.

There was someone present at the lunch who would have been the guest of honor if Luna had not been there. Oom Knorrig was this little old guy, incredibly cute and lovable, but not to be compared with our whale, of course. As far as I could gather, he was the oldest VanDwerg, or some kind of witch or wood-spirit, or the king of their tribe, or a rhymes-with-schmeprekon. Anyway, he was a big deal sort of person, with wisdom, and everybody respecting him.

"I wonder if Oom whatshisname might know anything about where we're trying to take Luna," Vern Chuckoff said.

"I was wondering the same thing," Maurice said.

Crazy in Poughkeepsie

"Let's get the Guru to ask him," I said. "They're both old wise guys, so they probably speak the same lingo."

37.

Guru Lumpo Smythe-Finkel, chewing on a toothpick, approached Oom Knorrig, the extremely adorable important personage. Oom Knorrig was sitting on a tree stump, just finishing a peach.

The Guru bowed to the Oom. The Oom jumped off the tree stump, tossed the peach pit over his shoulder, and bowed to the Guru.

The Guru took a stance, feet wide apart, knees bent.

The Oom took the same stance.

Then they both leapt straight up in the air, twisting in mid-leap, and landed back-to-back, facing away from one another. The Oom then bent forward, looking at the Guru between his legs, and wiggled his fingers at him.

In the same moment, the Guru lifted his left leg almost straight up, gripping his ankle with his left hand, and in that posture, spun so he was facing the between-the-legs finger-wiggling Oom.

Both of the sagacious beings then stood facing each other and jumped high in the air, once, twice, three times.

Villagers had dragged a chair into position behind the Guru, and he retired to it, and was handed a mug of tea. The Oom returned to his stump, and was given tea as well.

The two enlightened ones contemplated each other.

Then the Guru approached the Oom, and did a wide-legged dance, shifting his weight left, then right, then left again, spun around, clapped his hands, and extended his right hand, palm open, fingers pointing downward, to the Oom.

The Oom touched his index fingers, left and right, to the tip of his nose, stuck out his tongue, and rolled his eyes.

The Guru placed his left fist, thumb-side down, on top of his head, and made a back-handed flipping motion toward the Oom with his right hand, his fingertips brushing the underside of his chin.

Then the Oom made circles in the air with both hands.

The Guru grabbed one buttock with each hand and walked in a tiny circle.

Then the Oom reached behind his stump and produced a laptop computer. He flipped it open, the Guru approached, and the Oom showed him the screen.

Then the two spiritually advanced beings hugged, and walked off together to get some pie.

Crazy in Poughkeepsie

The Guru chose cherry pie, and the Oom had blueberry. Both had extra helpings of fresh cream on top.

38.

"So, what was all that with the Oom Knor-rig?" I asked the Guru.

"It's not far, and easy to get to. We'll start out in the morning."

"What did he show you on the laptop?"

"Map, what else?"

39.

And there we were, Cetarcadia, Mount Wha-lympus, Flukes of Glory, the place where good whales go, and they are all Good Whales. Naturally, the scale of the place was enormous. We stood, all of us, just inside the whaley pearly gates. We were stunned. I think even Luna was beyond impressed. There was a structure, a building, beside which the combined Taj Mahal, the Pyramids, the Louvre, and the Kremlin, all of Las Vegas, and midtown Manhattan would amount to a tiny garden shed or a temporary porta-potty. There was a dining room wherein little bald-headed human waiters with flat feet shuffled to and fro with platters of cheese blintzes, waffles, and blueberries in cream . . . merely for show, since the whales were ghostly and needed no food, and really, a single blintz would have been sufficient for all the ghostly occupants to sniff.

There was a godolympic-size swimming pool, which we came to understand was used by none of the occupants. It was just there so some of the whales could sun themselves beside it. They'd all had enough of swimming.

There were various amenities and amusements, a shuffleboard court the size of Chicago, gargantuan miniature golf, a horseshoe pitch—which I would have liked to have seen in use, with horseshoes the size of Volkswagens—but the aquatic mammal departed were not to be seen anywhere near these locations, which were just to set the tone of the place.

The big deal, the main attraction, the thing anyone would come to see, and where Luna as a deceased whale in good standing was entitled to be, was the meadow.

As to size, it was indescribable. Infinite. It would have to be, since every whale that ever lived, and died, was there, and all at the same time. There was sunshine, but not the sunshine we living mortals experience. This sunshine was better, brighter, warmer, and you could feel it love you. It enveloped, caroooed you. It carried you. That's how the light was. Then there was the fragrance. No wonder there weren't many customers to sniff the cheese blintzes. This was the smell of everything bright and good the mind of God could conceive. I don't think I should even try to describe the flowers, grass, weeds, even, except to say anyone, anyone at all, would consider it good luck to be able to study and live with a single blade of grass in that meadow. There was a sky. It was of a blue never seen on earth or by the living. There were clouds, fascinating clouds, each and every one the best cloud ever to exist.

That is where it happened. Now I have to try to describe what the happening was like. To begin with, if you had lived a long life in cold water, often in darkness, able to move around and even dance pretty well, but always conscious of a lot of gravity, and then found yourself in a place that was bright, and where you were weightless, your first impulse would be . . . to dance, I mean really dance, full-speed-ahead dance, leap-as-high-as-you-could dance, spin-and-flip-and-float-in-the-sky dance. That's what you'd do, and that's what the collected whales of the whole history of whale life were doing.

To dance right, you need music, and music there was . . . I didn't know where it came from, and I couldn't tell if I was hearing it with my ears or feeling it with my bones. All I knew was the music was in charge of me, and I was fine with that. At some point, I became dimly aware that I was hitting some excellent licks on my ghost flute. I was part of the band!

Lhasa and Luna joined the dance right away. Then the Guru, and then the rest of us. This was some kind of dancing! "Where's your bombinating now?" I thought. Besides moving in ways I had never imagined moving, I was having thoughts I'd never had, and seeing my own life and experiences in ways I had never seen them before. Also, I was close to understanding things I knew I wouldn't remember later, but they were important things, and just knowing I had almost understood them once would make me feel happy for as long as I lived.

We danced like that for maybe an hour, or it could have been a day, maybe a year, there was no way of telling. There came a time when the dancing stopped. It had to stop so we could have something to compare it to. The Guru, Lhasa, Molly, Vern and Maurice and I were all together, sitting on the wonderful, perfect grass.

"This is heaven, right?" I asked the Guru.

"What else could it be? But it's the whale heaven. It's heaven for whales."

"Is our heaven like this?"

"Don't know. I've never been. But based on what we're seeing here, I would venture a guess it's pretty good."

"You're going to tell me we can't stay here."

"It's for whales."

"Yes, but one of the whales is a close personal friend, and the dog likes it, and why can't we just stay?"

"Another thing is we are all alive. This is for whales who no longer are."

"Sure, but . . ."

"No buts about it. All you kids have to go back to Poughkeepsie."

"Don't even say that in a holy place!"

"Just the same, Maurice has to take his exams and get his degree. Molly has to fulfill her destiny, and you and Vern have to go to school."

"It's going to seem awfully dull."

"No, it won't. This little journey has opened you to stuff that was all around you, only you weren't able to see it."

"Such as what?"

"Well, bread, for a simple example. After the bread you had in Molly's village, you'll always experience it differently now that you've tasted the really good stuff. And, while it's not likely you'll ever see a live whale . . . though they do come up the river as far as Poughkeepsie, so it's not out of the question . . . anyway, you'll always look at whales with a different understanding than you could have had before."

"Bread and possible whale sightings doesn't sound that thrilling."

"Maybe not the best examples, but there are plenty of weird and unusual things right in your backyard. How does a place where flying saucers land strike you?"

"Flying saucers land in Poughkeepsie?"

"I didn't say they did, and I didn't say they didn't. You may want to look into it."

"How about you? You're coming back to Poughkeepsie, too, aren't you?"

"Just for a day or two. Then I'm catching a bus to the West. I made the acquaintance of a Native American shaman named Crazy Wig when I was traveling around, and he invited me to come and visit. There's going to be a mystical bowling tournament, and I'm thinking I might try my hand."

"But you're coming back after that, yes?"

"Maybe not right away. If I like it out west, I might stay and write a book about my experiences. I'll send you the manuscript, and you can correct the spelling mistakes and get it published for me."

"Why would you assume I would know how to do that?"

"Because I am your guru, and you are my pupil. I know you would never let me down."

"I happen to be a superior speller."

"By the way, the dog stays with you."

"Neat."

About the Author

Daniel Pinkwater is the author, and in some cases illustrator, of more than one hundred (and counting) beloved books, including *The Neddiad, Lizard Music, The Snarkout Boys and the Avocado of Death, Fat Men from Space, Borgel*, and picture books including the million-selling *The Big Orange Splot*. He illustrated many of his own books until that task passed to his wife, illustrator and novelist Jill Pinkwater, and other wonderful illustrators, including Tomie dePaola, James Marshall, D. B. Johnson, and Calef Brown. For twenty-five years, Pinkwater was a popular commentator on National Public Radio, and has been spotted on the pages of *The New York Times Magazine*, *The Washington Post*, *Saveur*, *OMNI*, and many other publications. He has received the Blue Ribbon for Fattest Author at the Dutchess County Fair five times.

Pinkwater lives with Jill, a world-class genius rough collie called The Peach, and certain cats in a centuries-old farmhouse in New York's Hudson River Valley.

About the Illustrator

Aaron Renier is the author of three graphic novels for younger readers: *Spiral-Bound, Walker Bean,* and *Walker Bean and the Knights of the Waxing Moon.* He is the recipient of the Eisner Award in 2006 for talent deserving of wider recognition, and was an inaugural resident for the Sendak Fellowship in 2010.